THE LARGE DOOR

Also by Jonathan Gibbs
Randall, or The Painted Grape

THE LARGE DOOR
BY JONATHAN GIBBS

BOILER HOUSE PRESS

"One of my fundamental assumptions is that
I have the power to seduce anyone."
Iris Murdoch

i.m. BB

"She let herself in, thinking about death."
Brigid Brophy, The Snow Ball

1

As in the manner of these things, Jenny had spent the weeks leading up to the trip resolutely avoiding doing any work whatsoever on her speech. Procrastination, she told her students often, is a skill well worth developing. It allows you to get a hundred small things done. And it gives the big things that remain a sense of scale that can only help focus the mind.

It wasn't like she hadn't started. She had notes, and she had a title – though in truth this was something she'd come up with more or less on the spot, when the conference organisers politely requested for the umpteenth time that she give them something they could put up online. 'Nothing is Settled: On Leonard Peters and the Subjunctive Mood' is what she had sent them, riffing on some old research on the ability of the subjunctive to suggest both contingency and desire, which she thought could be brushed up and made to take a turn upon the stage.

But this wasn't any old lecture, and the conference wasn't any old conference. This was the Festschrift event for

Leonard, her old supervisor and mentor, and – even after all these years – still one of the leading thinkers in the field. The two days were to be a celebration of him, of his career, and of his ongoing contribution to the discipline. And it was the job of her keynote speech – her of all people! – to round things off, and bring them to an appropriate conclusion. She should be appreciative, without gushing, or gushing, without fawning. Send everyone back out into the world brimming with knowledge and insight and confidence that they, as linguists, were doing good, necessary work, and that part of what they were doing was as a result of what Leonard Peters had done before them.

Only she hadn't written it.

She would finish it on the flight, she had told herself. Not that it had ever quite reached the stage of telling. She had simply understood herself, as if by telepathy, batting the thought away whenever it threatened to arise, like you might bat away a small annoying insect: repeatedly, untiringly, never-quite-successfully. Up there, at 35,000 feet, lifted far beyond the reach of her usual cares and concerns (she was flying premium economy, courtesy of the conference organisers) she would be able to put her thoughts in order. No, more than that: they would fall, themselves, into an order that, down here on the ground, she could neither anticipate nor conceive of. They would drop into place as they might in a dream.

So it was that Jenny stood in the middle of the bedroom of her Oakland condo, glaring at her suitcase. She had her fingers pressed to her temples, and from her closed mouth there came a high, distant keening sound, as if she had an angry bee trapped in there. The cab would be here in half an hour to take her to the airport, and she was breathless with frustration and self-recrimination. She should have flown earlier. Or she should have finished the lecture days ago, weeks ago. She shouldn't have accepted the invitation. She shouldn't have come to America in the first place, flapping in the slipstream of a faithless man. Shouldn't have taken the job at Berkeley, fluke though it was, miracle though it was. She should have stayed in England, should have stayed at home in bed, with the covers pulled firmly over her head.

She stared now at the suitcase, set open on the bed, now around at the rest of the room. You might have thought she was trying to work out if she could fit the one into the other. Nor was this such a ludicrous idea. The room, after all, had come out of the case, more or less. She had been in California a little over three years, and the condo, pleasant though it was, in a well-designed and friendly development, still had the feel of a holiday let. She had brought no furniture with her from the wreckage of her marriage back east, still less from her life before that. On the walls there was barely a poster; there was nothing growing in the low square concrete tubs on her balcony, nothing displayed on the living room shelving but books and more books. This was what she had to show for her forty years on god's green earth.

Jenny raised her hands and clapped them over her head – paf! pa-paf-paf! – until she recalled what it was she'd been trying to remember. Her tablet. God, she hated her tablet: hated it. She deepened her keening to a low warning growl and scoured the room until she saw it, lying under a pile of books on the floor. On the tablet were a dozen academic papers she needed to read, plus fifty more she had needed to read at some point in the past but hadn't. There was a book chapter to proofread and a journal issue waiting for her editor's foreword, and there were two full-length student dissertations for doctoral examinations she had scheduled in the weeks after the conference. The tablet was her own personal black hell-pit of despair. It held in one convenient place the entirety of what she couldn't bear to face. She had fantasies about being mugged, and screeching at her mugger, here take my tablet... holding it out to him, thrusting it into his hands. Take the fucking thing. She knelt down and slid it out from the pile, then crossed to the bed and shoved it in her handbag.

Into the handbag, too, went headphones, nail buffers, cigarettes. Into the suitcase: a pair of blue jeans, some black trousers, a second sweater – it was February, and the temperature in Amsterdam was a shocking five degrees Celsius. Into the bag: cables and adaptors. Into the case: tights, bras, socks and knickers, rifled from the underwear drawer, plus an extra pair of pants and tights for her handbag. Some of her underwear, she realised as she pawed through it, actually predated her arrival in the States. She pulled the drawer all the way out and performed a quick triage, balling old knickers and throwing them at the bin by the door. She imagined the kind of underwear that would unfurl in mid-air and float wispily to the ground halfway to its destination. None of these was that kind of underwear. These flew hard and straight and true: one, two, three direct hits, thup thup thup.

The state of her underwear drawer gave her pause, and she stood there, hands wrist-deep in undies, and closed her eyes.

'Fuck it,' she said.

She went to her wardrobe and knelt to shift boxes and bags, until she found one particular box. In it, half-covered by tissue paper, was a pair of knee-length black leather boots. She pinched back the paper and touched the leather of the boots, tenderly, like you might touch a bruise, feeling for their sheen, for a sense of their former glory. She would be seeing Frankie at the conference. Seeing her, properly, for the first time since her move to the US – since her retreat, her flight, since her grand evasion. Her stomach tightened, and for a moment she felt as if she might vomit.

She pulled the boots from the box onto her lap. She needed to find love again, in some form: reintroduce it, in some measure, into her life. Still holding the boots, she stood up and looked about her. That is what her bedroom told her – and the view, too, through the window onto the bright shared courtyard garden, with its gravel beds, its salmon paving and its fat, sprinkler-fed palms. That was their considered advice. And Jenny, whose mother had worked in an architect's practice, and whose father had been a goods buyer in a nationwide department store, knew better than to ignore the advice of the built environment.

Nor was finding love beyond her capabilities. She had the power to seduce anyone, was her quiet but firmly held belief. It was merely a question of what it might take. She walked stiff-backed to the bed and put the boots in the case, removing a pair of loafers, a jacket and a terrible – really a *terrible*, ugly and plain – cardigan to make space for them. She pressed them down and shored them about with bras and knickers until they stayed put. Lying there, doubled up against themselves, they looked twice as sexy, as if being folded and confined added a strain of perversity to their native glamour. Frankie would be there in Amsterdam. She would see her, be with her, there at the conference. Frankie was the opening speaker, she the closing one. There was a symmetry there. Who knew what might happen?

Biting her lip and working quickly so she would not cry, Jenny pulled out from under the packed clothes the internal straps and stretched them over the contents until they met and could be clipped together. She lifted over and closed the lid, and, when it wouldn't zip shut, climbed onto the bed and then right on top of the case, sitting on it and squashing it down. Reaching between her legs, she pulled the zip first along the remainder of this side, then this one, then this, and then it was done. She stayed there for a moment, breathing heavily, feet set broadly on the eiderdown, wobbling a little as her weight shifted, for all the world like a pope perched on his inflatable throne. She scanned the room for anything she might have missed, might have forgotten. The room ignored her gaze; it turned its head aside. Go, it seemed to say. Go to Holland. Go to Frankie. Go to Europe. But don't think you will be missed. And do not think you will be able to return, just like that, as if nothing had happened, if you do not get what you want.

On the flight she drank her G&T, skimmed the on-demand films, read twenty pages of the book she had bought at the airport before deciding it bored her, with its divorced, depressed, elaborately uncharismatic detective, and reached with a sigh for her laptop. The file for Leonard had a word count of 852, but much of this was biographical detail cut and pasted from other documents. The few personal anecdotes, now that she scrolled through them, seemed inconclusive and incomprehensible. The things she remembered, in general, were so random, were such incidental scraps of the past – such as you might imagine seeing float down over half the country from a plane blown up in midair – that it felt wrong to set store by them.

The truth was that the Leonard she thought of now, as she rattled the ice in her plastic glass, and looked out at the dark mass of America – for she had succeeded in not thinking about him for a long time, as she had not thought about Frankie, not thought, really, about England at all – was not Leonard the eloquent professor, holding forth from the lectern, nor the meeting room Leonard of the frazzled brow and puckered lips, that bespoke an acute impending crisis of thought, nor even the avuncular conference Leonard, who always seemed to pull from some obscure budgetary pocket the money to pick up the bill for booze and food on the last night. No, the Leonard that rose up before her now, somewhere over Idaho, was the Leonard who had asked her to go to bed with him, that one time. Or not even asked, really, but obliquely indicated his wish to do so. The Leonard whom she turned down when he drunkenly – probably – courageously – probably – and regretfully – definitely – propositioned her that one time. Which he never did again. He was most considerate about it.

She'd told her husband about it once, she remembered, and he'd found it funny, so she supposed she must have meant for it to be funny, in the telling. When she thought of it now, nearly twenty years on, her response was not even one of anger towards Leonard, particularly, but of curiosity about herself, why she insisted on thinking of this when she thought of him. Had it been a one-off, a momentary misstep? Or had he been like this all along, and this was just the one time the mask slipped? They'd worked so closely for so long, and he'd taught her so much, had been so generous with his time and encouragement and influence. He hadn't got her the job, there in the English department at Manchester – her first full-time post – but it was his teaching, his guidance throughout her PhD, that had given her skills to get it. There had been an intellectual connection, and a personal one. He'd taught her stuff. Perhaps she'd cured him of it, the coming on to junior members of staff. Perhaps that was what she'd taught him in return.

He'd been not long divorced at the time, after fifteen years – fifteen! – of marriage, and had reached an age of, she was beginning to understand now, in her forty-second year, strange and desperate disorientation. It was Christmas, or nearly, with the term done, and a brief period of respite upon them before marking deadlines kicked in. Perhaps it had just come over him, the animal need to pitch yourself forward, reach after something – to steady yourself: see if it will hold you, keep you upright; or if not then to take out and obliterate the very thing you hoped would hold you. To fall, definitely and comprehensively, with all the self-awareness and self-knowledge of the tragic hero or professional clown.

She remembered the room where it had happened, not in the university, but someone's home – the coldness and darkness of a university town with the students gone – a Christmas drinks with maybe fifteen or twenty attendees. Awkwardness was the default setting for such occasions, the only other possible settings being genial inebriation and galloping calamity. You wanted it to be over, so you drank to speed the time, but the more you drank, the longer you stayed, and further the end of the night receded before you. Well-oiled was the phrase people used to use to describe someone publicly drunk, but that wasn't right, she thought. It isn't that the machine is lubricated, and so operates more smoothly, but that the parts – the nuts and bolts and cogs and wheels – become loosened. A well-oiled machine will still run, but one with loosened parts risks falling to pieces altogether, shooting crucial cogs and sprockets across the carpet.

In her memory, she had left the living room, where people stood in cringing groups, uncirculating, to hide out for a moment in a room at the far end of the hallway, which she supposed must have been the music room. It had an upright piano, lid raised to show its nicotined teeth, along with various instrument cases and music stands. The inadequate shelving bowed under decades' worth of vinyl records and musical scores. She'd placed herself so you'd think she was browsing them, and was sipping from a glass of water she had brought with her, to give herself a break from the wine. She had been there no more than a minute when someone came into the room.

It was Leonard. He had in each hand a glass of red wine. From between the fingers of one extended a lit cigarette.

'Hello Leonard,' she said.

'Hello,' he'd replied. 'I guessed you wanted to get away from us miserable old bastards, so I came to spoil it for you. I've brought you this.' He held out a glass.

'So you have.'

She took the glass. Now she had a glass in each hand, one wine and one water.

'You've been admiring the library?' said Leonard, who

she now saw was more drunk than she'd realised, earlier, talking to him in the main room. His words and movements were fluid, but also precipitate. He was at once bouncing on the balls of his feet and somehow also weaving on the spot, like one of those battery-operated flowers in pots with sunglasses on their faces, that certainly didn't exist then, and probably don't now, but that during their brief moment of faddish ubiquity danced in time to any music you might play in their hearing.

'Yes, well,' she said, imperiously. 'That was the plan. I've not really had the chance as yet.'

She went to take a drink from the wine glass, as if to expiate her boldness, but found, when it touched her lips, that it was the glass with water in, so she lowered it and raised the other and drank from that, but drank from it in her confusion as if it were water, tipping back her head and glugging so the wine made her cough.

'Let me take that,' he said, stepping in towards her. Only he didn't. He didn't take the glass. Instead he put his hand around her wrist – not tightly, or forcefully; you might almost say without intent – and held it there, while he swayed, smiling. He was not tall, Leonard, and in her party heels Jenny was near enough level with him, eye to watery eye.

'Let me take that,' he said again, and she stared at him, breathless from the coughing, in what must have looked something like surprise. She wanted him at least to take the glass, so he'd have to leave hold of her wrist.

Then, as if he'd been waiting for one particular moment in the looped trajectories of his swaying circuits, he pounced: in a rapid series of movements he let go of her wrist, took her water glass and put it and his own wine glass down on the flat top lid of the piano, then got his left hand back around her right wrist and with his right hand took her left elbow. They stood there for a moment, saying nothing, as if they were stood on a dance floor, waiting for the orchestra to strike up.

'Jennifer,' he said, and leaned in.

'Jenny, please,' she insisted, turning her head aside, and snorting at herself, for the sheer inanity of her words, and her behaviour. 'I mean, Leonard, please. You don't have to call me Jennifer.'

As he bore down on her – though there was no down about it; he simply closed the gap between them, tugging her bodily towards him as he pushed his face towards hers – he did in fact begin to overbalance, so that she found she had to brace herself to keep them both upright. The polished floorboards made her shoe slip a little. This hadn't happened before. Nothing like it had happened. Not that there hadn't been plenty of opportunities: friendly pints in the pub after work; being the last people on their corridor still in when everyone else had gone home; trips to conferences, at home and abroad. It was the fact that it had never happened, when she had in truth sometimes worried that it might, that made it such a surprise, there in the music room of a university colleague whose name was now lost to oblivion.

Where a moment before they'd looked like they were about to begin a waltz, now they were more positioned as for a tango. She still had her wine glass in her left hand, and as his face loomed for what was presumably intended as a kiss she turned her head to the side and brought up her glass, straining against the downward pressure of his hand on her arm to get it to her mouth.

She got the glass to her mouth, and drank, and that gave her confidence – both for the fact that having a glass at her mouth meant he couldn't kiss her, and, more generally, that if she was having a drink of wine then everything was perfectly normal. This was a drinks party, and here she was, having a drink, with a senior colleague. She may even have made some fatuous comment on the quality of the wine, keeping the glass meanwhile hovering in front of her face.

Then, emboldened by having halted Leonard in his sloppy prelude to a kiss, she herself set in train a series of movements. She pushed and twisted and stepped, again, almost as if these were the moves of a dance, in such a way as to get herself out from under Leonard, and free of his double grip, but leaving him at the same time more or less balanced. She ended up a couple of feet from him, further down the piano, with Middle C between them, and the fingers of her left hand resting on the bass keys, as if ready to sound a thunderous alarm. Her wine glass was in her right hand. Her feet were in the third position. Her face was blushing, and her eyes were comely and bright.

'So, Leonard,' she said, in a way that she hoped would draw a line under the last ninety seconds, if not erase them altogether.

But he stood and swayed and narrowed his eyes and said, in a low voice entirely unlike his own, that, she had thought, later that night, as she removed her heels and tights, sitting on her bed in her small Rusholme house, had been, despite everything, rich with what sounded like genuine passion, 'Jenny, come on...' The 'come on' was both a general, between-adults plea to give over with the peevish, teenaged behaviour, and a specific and direct appeal to come now with him somewhere properly private.

Thinking back on it, she had felt overwhelmingly angry and confused, but now, as she tapped the plastic airline glass against her teeth, with her long-haul socks pulled up her calves and her laptop warm and useless as a cat on her knees, the thought of him there, then, made her want to laugh. He had been entirely ridiculous, with his lefty beard and his flyaway hair: never particularly stylish, it had got increasingly unkempt in the months following the divorce. He must have known he was being ridiculous, she thought. Worse than being ridiculous, he was being *inept*, and Leonard was one of the most *apt* people she knew.

If he knew it, why did he persevere? For he did. Even when she had told him to stop, he came back with it, one last time: 'Come on, Jenny,' he'd said. So that in the end she had actually said, 'What? What, Leonard? What exactly is it that you are proposing?' And the thought of the look on his face made her snort, again, there on the plane, and think of how, the day after tomorrow, she would have to stand on stage and talk about him, in all seriousness, to a roomful of colleagues and admirers, for forty-five minutes, with him right there in front of her. She felt moved to wipe her eye, as if to remove a tear, though no tear was there.

So far as she knew, he'd never done it again. His name hadn't ever come up on the whisper network of pricks and dickheads to keep an eye on, and stay out of otherwise empty lifts with. Perhaps, with Leonard, it really had been just the once. Or, perhaps, just her. They'd neither of them mentioned it again, but something went out of the relationship all the same. Which made her angry. It was his fault they couldn't get along like they had before. Why did he have to spoil it? But still: what an idiot, what a fool, what a balloon he'd been. Poor lurching Leonard. She imagined herself up there, on stage, halfway through her address, diverting into that anecdote. 'Let me tell you about one time, I remember, with Leonard.' She closed her eyes and held her glass to her lip, tipped back her head and smiled in strong delight.

2

Lieve walked barefoot into the kitchen and yawned. She put her phone flat on the table and went to open cupboards and drawers to fetch out the breakfast things. She moved as in a dream, but as in a dream she knew well. A recurrent dream. From the cupboard: a bowl, a glass, granola, a jar of honey, a spoon. From the fridge: yoghurt, juice, berries. The things made their particular noises, as they did every morning. The high short note of the spoon in the bowl, the throaty gulp of the juice as it poured from the cartoon, like it was drinking itself. Her movements were practised enough to be efficient, efficient enough to be elegant. The tune of a song was in her head, that she could not place, while outside it was becoming light, the buildings ghosting into familiarity against the ever-strange sky. She folded shut the spout on the juice carton and addressed the room, speaking in English.

'Thank you very much. My name is Lieve Braam, and I am a doctoral student here at the University of Amsterdam.' She spooned yoghurt into the bowl, then added berries, tilting the plastic tray and tapping the bottom to tip them in one by one. 'Doctoral student,' she said again, altering the angle of attack of that first vowel, trying to sound less Dutch. 'Doctoral student.' She shook in granola, then dug out some honey and held it high over the food so it descended in a thick translucent cord through the air. She drew slow golden spirals over the granola and berries; then, when the cord had thinned almost to nothing, she tweaked the spoon back up to true and sucked it clean in her mouth, upside-down on her tongue.

She walked with the bowl over to the window and looked out. A blackbird was hopping about on the wooden table on her tiny roof terrace. There was an old tin tray where she sometimes left out breadcrumbs and other scraps, but just now it was empty. The cold of the air could be felt through the glass. There was a haze of condensation on the pane, and a miniature pool of water sat on the white wooden sill; it held itself shunted up against the glass, packed tight within its meniscus.

'My name is Lieve Braam,' she said to the bird. 'And I am a doctoral student here at the University of Amsterdam. For my PhD I am studying the etiquette of transnational business communication in Indo-European and Asian languages. Which is, I promise you, more fun than it sounds.'
A pause for laughter. 'Today I am going to share with you...'

The rest of her sentence became lost as she spooned more of her breakfast into her mouth, speaking and eating at once, so the words became jumbled up with the food and lost all form. The bird grew bored and flew off.

She swallowed, unperturbed, and went on: 'In a moment I am going to ask you to turn to the person next to you...'

Her phone pinged.

It was Mysha, of course it was. The message read, in Dutch:

Yeah so G texted me this morning apologising. The usual crap. We're basically finished I think. So bored of this.

Lieve put down her spoon and bowl to thumb out her answer.

Too bad. But overdue imo.

Yeah, overdue and timely.

Lieve paused, thumbs held over the screen. Mysha was the only person she communicated with to any significant extent like this, on social media, and she wasn't always confident she could express herself with 100% accuracy. Spoken and written language involved not just lexis and syntax, but also gesture, context and intonation, and digital communication was no different: it offered a thousand ways to misspeak, to misconstrue and be misconstrued.

Lieve wrote back: Forget him. Focus on what's important. You ready?

The three dots appeared to show that Mysha was typing, but then disappeared. Lieve drank some juice. When she looked again, the message was there.

Absolutely. By which I mean absolutely shitting myself. I'm going to crash and burn. You'll kill it, though, bitch. She signed off with three smiley emojis with hearts for eyes.

Lieve lifted her eyes and made a small, private sound of exasperation. There were seven years between Mysha and her, and although she liked her friend a lot, she wished she would grow up a little. That was if she even had the capacity to grow up. Which, honestly, just now, she doubted. Had *she* been like this when she was twenty-three? She almost crossed herself at the thought. In any case, there was no question but that Mysha would be like this when she was thirty, when she was forty, fifty, sixty. She'd be like it when she was a grandmother.

You'll be fine, she replied. Just remember: speak slowly, like we practised. Make eye contact. We'll all be rooting for you. See you later.

Mysha came back with an emoji of a cat's face. Lieve stared at it. The cat had scared eyes and it held its paws up to its open mouth. It reminded her of Edvard Munch's painting The Scream, but she had no idea if this was an intentional reference. This was the other problem with social media: not just that online language was as intricately ambiguous as its spoken or written iterations, but that it evolved at a far faster rate. Idioms and catchphrases went through their lifecycle ten, twenty times faster than they ever did in the playground or the office, like viruses adapting to outpace antibiotics. It made what she did difficult. Linguistics had got in the habit of describing language two ways: synchronically and dia-chronically – as a snapshot of a stable, existing state, and as a process evolving over time. Looking at the angstful cat face on her phone screen, Lieve wondered if this distinction had become impossible to maintain.

She sat at the table and finished her breakfast, scrolling through the conference schedule on the university website with little yoghurty swipes of her finger, pausing to compare times and adjudicate clashes. It was just gone eight o'clock, and although registration wasn't till nine thirty she wanted to be there early.

And yes, she did hope that she would, as Mysha put it, kill it.

Killing it was a big part of her plan.

She was in the last year of her PhD and this was the first big international conference she'd spoken at. Jaap, her supervisor, had basically organised it, together with the British contingent representing Leonard Peters. Jaap was introducing her session, and he'd as good as promised her he'd persuaded a bunch of people to come along to hear her. Half the names listed in her bibliography were going to be there, if you believed him: Dominique Brayard, Jennifer Thursley, Mehmet Golat. And yet here she was, preparing to spring some kindergarten nonsense on them. The kind of stuff that worked brilliantly in business seminars, but risked majorly pissing off academics, who weren't generally that hot on role-play and self-reflection. *In a moment I would like you to turn to the person next to you and introduce yourself.* If anyone was going to crash and burn, it was her.

Her phoned pinged. A photo, this time.

It was a mirror-selfie of Mysha in skinny black trousers, a pale pink top Lieve hadn't seen before and her cropped camel-coloured leather jacket. She was turned slightly sideways and was holding the jacket with her free hand just below the lapels. The trousers, naturally, were tight as hell, and the jacket ended just above her bum. She did look very cute. She also looked entirely inappropriate for giving a paper at a conference.

What do you think? read the caption. Then, a moment later, came another message. This is option 1 btw.

Then:

Plan B is go. Remember we're going clubbing after. And an emoji of a man and woman dancing.

'Fuck.' Lieve tossed the phone onto the table. Mysha had a long-running joke whereby she referred to Jaap Vos, who was her supervisor as well as Lieve's, as her 'Plan B' – even as 'Plan A' changed from one bloody useless arsehole boyfriend to the next. Jaap was a great teacher, forever sparking new directions in Lieve's thinking, but she doubted these attributes figured very highly in Mysha's assessment of him. And, yes, Mysha had made sure that she had invited him to the unofficial nightclub excursion organised by the students for after the evening's formal activities were done. She was an idiot, thought Lieve – but at least she was an idiot with a plan.

Option two, when it came, was a red skirt and floral blouse. The pose was equally coquettish: face on, left knee forward and the other hip pushed out to the side; her right elbow cocked and her hand on the waist. Her shoulder was lifted and she was half pouting, half blowing a kiss. Lieve shook her head and replied that option one looked good, signing off with a kiss emoji and a see-you-later, then cleared away her breakfast and got herself ready to go.

It was indeed cold out. Even on the walk to the tram stop she was glad to have her hat and gloves. She pulled the hat – a neat woollen beanie – tight down over her ears. She liked the way it rubbed against the fuzz of her hair. She'd got the buzz-cut a few months into her Master's degree, three years ago now, and had kept it ever since. It had made her feel more like a student, more fully divorced from her previous life. Mysha, who had started at the same time as her, had been appalled. She'd said she looked like a Holocaust survivor. *A beautiful one*, she'd said, *but still*. Not that this stopped Mysha begging to be allowed to use the clippers on Lieve's hair herself when it needed doing.

Jaap, too, had teased her for it. 'You'll have to let it grow when you finish here,' he'd said. 'They don't want hipsters working in the big consultancies.'

'Oh, they do,' she'd answered. 'I'm exactly the kind of

hipster they want. Looks edgy as fuck, but works fucking hard.'

She stood in the tram, looking at her reflection in the dark glass of the closed door and thinking about emojis: the cat face, the blown kiss. She allowed herself to swing with the tram's movement, twisting her hand in the thick looped plastic strap of the handle. There are however many muscles in the face – we are capable of a hundred different expressions – but when we need to make a point clearly we rely on just a few, and those we use we exaggerate. Lieve pouted at herself, aping Mysha's expression, letting her ring and stud dig touches of light into the glass. She was wearing trousers pleated at the waist, with a crease ironed down the front, and lace-up shoes, still new enough to be smart. Under her coat was a shirt with neat little collars, and a round-necked sleeveless sweater. No jacket.

She had a vision of Mysha, gyrating like a pole-dancer, with one hand on the lectern, as she mouthed the words of her paper. She turned to hide her smile, and looked out through the other doors. There, too, there was her pale reflection, hovering over the city streets, the brightening sky. She set her face and looked through herself, at the people walking, on bicycles, the cars. *I am a doctoral student here at the University of Amsterdam. Today I will be presenting some of my research into the transnational aspects of business etiquette in the Indo-European languages. Which is, I promise you, more fun than it sounds.* Pause for laughter. *In a moment I am going to ask you to turn to the person next to you and introduce yourself.*

Jenny was roused from fretful sleep by the muffled fuss of her phone, sounding from somewhere among the bedcovers. She

groaned and cast blindly about until she found and successfully doused it. The day hadn't even begun, and yet here she
was, already spent. She had slept a bit on the plane, but when
she had lain down on the hotel bed, after checking in and
showering, she had fallen straight into a sleep as sheer and
deep as a chasm in the ocean floor. She opened her eyes and
gathered herself, then let out a pitiful wail – ow-wow-waaaah,
she said, like a fractious child, arms flung out wide and gap-
ing her mouth at the ceiling. She went on saying it long past
the point of reasonable curiosity. This is what people did who
lived alone, she thought. And she had lived alone too long.
She needed to let love back into her life. She carried on making the pathetic noise until her mouth dried shut.

She shrugged off the hotel dressing gown and stood in
her underwear before the wardrobe, already ranged with
the clothes she had brought with her. For tomorrow's talk, a
pinstripe boot-cut trouser suit. For mooching, her jeans and
jumpers. For today, a collared grey woollen dress that had
just leapt out at her from a shop window in Rockridge only
a matter of weeks before. Her Get Frankie dress. She pulled
on a slip, then the dress, straightening with a little jump so
it fell down around her hips. It was to her mind a beguil-
ing mix of the puritan and the slinky: rich in New England
genes and warm to the touch. And the colour of it, oh the
colour of it was the colour of the sky over the Atlantic when it
threatened rain. How could it fail? She checked herself in the
mirror, rising and falling on the balls of her feet as she did
up the last buttons, then pressed the twin white prongs of
the pointy collar against her collar bones to tease them flat.

Doing her face was slow work. It was as if she was having
to reach through a tunnel of jetlag to make every mark. She

leaned in at the dressing table mirror and scowled. Leaned back and bared her teeth. Raised and lowered her chin, so as to expose herself to maximum scrutiny. She thought of art restorers working on ancient frescoes, the emulsions and enzymes they might apply with their tiny brushes to mitigate the depredations of time. But the flaking she saw in the mirror, these specks and splotches, this thinning of the dermis, the loss of elasticity, none of these could be remediated, but only distracted from, like a stage magician used his patter to cloak the real workings of his act.

She touched corrector in at the insteps of her eyes, then added shadow, feeling her fingertips drag on the skin of the lids. She turned her head this way and that, keeping herself always in sight. The aim was to catch yourself with the kind of careless, uncommitted glance which was the most that the majority of people would ever settle on you. To see only the momentary effect, not the scaffolding. Fatigue dogged her hand as Jenny held the mascara brush half an inch from her lashes, her mouth hanging dumbly open. The decisive moment could never be second-guessed. It was a gamble of consciousness and will. There, and there. Done.

She pulled on her tights and then pulled on her boots, flexing her knees and toes to get her feet to the ends. The black leather of them caught and cupped the light in the sleek folds that ran all the way from the ankle to the calf. She stood and considered herself again in the mirror. Then she lifted both hands and in a single sweeping movement threw her hair back over her shoulders, left and right together. Finally she adjusted her fringe. God, she hated her fringe. Sylvia Plath was the look she'd been after, when she'd last had her hair properly styled, which had been soon after

arriving on the east coast with her new and unexpected husband. It had been intended as a tribute of sorts to the spirit
of America, but in truth Sylvia Plath always looked rather
plain, and Jenny was older now than Plath had ever been. If
the plainness was a disguise, as it might have been for Plath,
it was, for Jenny, altogether too effective.

She fixed her earrings – pearls, a gift from Frankie – gathered her things and headed downstairs.

As she swung on the turns of the banister, her dress moving around her legs and her bag lifting in a brief dream of
weightlessness from her side, she thought about what might
be waiting for her downstairs. She knew that Frankie and
Leonard were both staying in this same hotel, a boutique
outfit fifteen minutes' walk from the university buildings,
but she had – appallingly – not been in contact with either of
them ahead of time. She explained this to herself with reference to her never-ending avalanche of work, and the fun it
would be to surprise them, but she knew in her heart it was
gutless and unforgivable. The invitation to give the closing
address must have come, in some way, from Frankie. She
would have been deeply involved in its planning. As such,
it felt like an olive branch, entirely underserved: an offering
that Jenny, the ingrate, had brushed aside.

On one of the landings she caught a view of herself in a
tabletop mirror and stopped to take a final look at herself.
She rested her coat on a chair back, pulled and twisted her
hair up and fixed it with a clip so it lay in a sort of loose pony-
tail folded flat across the back of the top of her head. It felt
right to be here: to see Frankie again, at last, and to celebrate
Leonard. Let the spotlight fall on his work. Let him bask in
it, the poor old sod, for what other pleasures remained for

him, really? Leonard Peters, she would say, and she would mean it, is a giant of linguistics. As we look back over the rich and varied landscape of his career, I have the honour and the pleasure of asking you all to join with me...

She fussed at her fringe again, then gave up on it and took her coat back up. She set off, at a slower pace, for the stairs were steep in this beautiful hotel set in an Amsterdam town house, with oil paintings in gilt frames, and pieces of Delft pottery sitting pert on their pedestals, but when she came to the ground floor, and turned into the dining room where breakfast was laid out, and saw them there, around their table, she stopped altogether.

She stood on the threshold, watching through the doorway.

There they were, three of them, the only people present. The room was poised, pristine, with cloths on the tables, china cups parked on saucers, individual tulips in small clear-glass vases; there was the smell of coffee and bread. But there was no sound, no movement.

There was Leonard and there Frankie, and another woman she didn't recognise. The two women standing, Leonard sitting. Jenny had caught them, in fact, in the act of finishing and readying themselves to go.

Frankie, on the left of the tableau, had a forefinger resting on a piece of paper laid on the table. Her chin was folded down into her neck and she had a disdainful look on her face that Jenny found both funny and, because it was so character-istic, entirely loveable. Leonard was leaning forward, hands on the table, preparing to push himself up from it, while the unknown woman, on the right, was glancing sideways at him with an expression of something like concern.

There was a stillness about the scene, and it carried within it an air of melancholy, almost, that took Jenny aback. It was like when you caught a clock between ticks, when there was just enough time before the second hand moved again for you to think that it might have stopped altogether. She felt herself looking at them, and wondered what it was she was seeing.

Then the moment was released.

It unfurled itself, and Leonard did in fact push himself to standing. As he did so, he caught sight of Jenny, and his face broke open in an expression of delight, which then changed to one of feigned hurt.

'Jenny,' he said. An admonishment as much as a greeting.

Jenny responded with a wave, and began to make her way towards them, while Leonard came around the side of the table to meet her, Frankie taking a delicate step back to let him past. He stood with his hands in his side jacket pockets, the thumbs out and pointing forwards. Also characteristic: it was the pose she would have pulled if she had wanted, for instance, to impersonate him.

'Good god,' he said, and he wiggled his tremendous eyebrows. 'How long were you there, spying on us?'

She ignored his question. 'How are you, Leonard?' she said, seriously.

Now that she was standing in front of him, she realised how old he looked. Of course he did; Frankie did, too. Or, no: she looked older, compared to how Jenny remembered her. Leonard looked absolutely, unequivocally old. But what was he – seventy? Not even that – he was still in his sixties, surely? It was as if his cheeks and jawline had been sucked back into his face, leaving the nose and chin badly exposed as the baggage they were. Brazenly ignoring Frankie – she couldn't even bring herself to look at her, though her face, she knew, was burning – Jenny stuck out her hand to Leonard.

He took his right hand slowly from his jacket pocket and moved it towards hers. As he did so, he leaned back and lifted his chin, as if so as to direct his gaze at her from somewhere that little bit further away.

'Well, well,' he said. And then, 'Jenny Thursley. I'm well enough, I suppose. And how are you?'

They stood there for a moment, joined at the hand, but the hands not moving; and, as earlier at the door, she had the sense of seeing the moment she was part of from the outside, of the moment being cast into somebody else's perspective. As if, when you shook someone by the hand, everything else stopped, which in a sense it did.

He let go of her hand and introduced her to the woman stood next to him.

'Deborah, you know Jenny, don't you? Jenny Thursley. Jenny, Deborah is the secretary of the ISPL.'

'Of course.'

The two women exchanged quick banal pleasantries, talking over each other. But – Deborah regretfully gestured to her watch – it seemed they were pressed for time. There was a car waiting outside.

'We could offer you a lift,' Leonard said. 'But we do have to go.'

Jenny demurred, and said she'd stay and have some breakfast. She could make her own way to the conference. In fact, she thought, it was so short a distance that she did wonder why they'd bothered with a car at all. More than this, though, she was confused by the whole exchange. She needed time to think it through, to tease out the implications. She was annoyed with herself for offering her hand to Leonard. Why had she not simply embraced him, as she had done a hundred times before? It wasn't because of how she'd been thinking of Leonard on the flight, she thought. This was not that Leonard.

He took his leave: slowly, oldly. Deborah at his side.

Frankie remained. After the brief fit of activity, the room was still once more, and Jenny was happy to be able to just look at her. She was older, yes, but no less radiant. Her hair was whiter, with a short blunt nub of a quiff that served as a neat reminder of her more radical years. She still had a boxy, either-way-up look about her face, that went with her fitted jacket and shirt, but all this, Jenny knew, was at odds with the facts of her body.

'Come here till I kiss you,' Jenny said. She put her hand on Frankie's arm, and leaned in. She tried not to notice that Frankie was wearing no significant pieces of jewellery; tried not to see if Frankie had noticed her wearing her pearls. In her boots Jenny had inches of height on her, but Frankie had never been one to be cowed.

Frankie moved her face in in response, but moved to the side as she did, so they met mouth to cheek and cheek to mouth.

'That's not a kiss,' Jenny said, comically, through squashed lips.

'It will have to do, for now.'

'But god it's good to see you. How are you?'

'Fine. And it's good to see you, too. How are you?'

Jenny looked at her quizzically. Something about how the question was phrased surprised her, as if Frankie wasn't asking what Jenny thought she was asking.

'I'm absolutely knackered, frankly. I've been, as you can imagine, completely avoiding doing any thinking at all about this whole thing. And now I'm in a complete tizz over tomorrow. What am I going to say? I can't even think.'

'It'll be fine. You'll be fine.'

'That's easy for you to say. Your talk is in, what, an hour? It's practically done.'

Frankie smiled.

A glance to the door.

'You've got to go.'

'I have. You do know what time it starts, right?'

'You know me. I'll be there. I just won't be, well, *early*. But, Frankie. I'll see you, properly? You're not shooting off as soon as you're done?'

'Of course not. And of course you will.'

Frankie took Jenny's hand and clasped it in hers. She squeezed it and swayed it gently from side to side.

'Properly.'

'Yes, properly. Come on, now. Sit down.' She half-led her towards the table. 'Have the omelette. It's very good.'

Jenny did as she was told. When the waiter came to take her order she was still beaming with such unbridled joy that he thought her smile was for him, and blushed as he bent to gather the dirty plates, and she blushed, for him, for why should she not? It was a free world, and she had the power to seduce anyone she chose, anyone at all.

3

The walk to the university did indeed take less than ten minutes. It was cold, after California, but the air was bright, through and through, promising clarity to come. The strong low light boomed along the canal and cast up thin rippling lines of gold to dance on the undersides of the bridges. The people walking towards her on the cobbled canal-side roadway were transformed by the oncoming sun into slim alien silhouettes, faceless and nearly bodiless, with blurred accents of gold to their shoulders and arms, and a furze-like nimbus to their head. Jenny walked phone in gloved hand, the other hand gloveless for touching, looking down then up as she went, squinting, having forgotten to bring sunglasses with her.

She enjoyed the ubiquity of the cyclists, their happy practical sense of possessing the streets, the way they moved in long thin flights down their designated lanes, like migrating birds, and the way that cars and pedestrians both stopped to let them pass. The bikes, too, had a Spartan grace compared to the over-designed techno-monsters people rode back home. No lycra, no high-vis vests, no helmet-mounted cameras. They and their riders made of Amsterdam a carousel catwalk of coats, gloves, scarves and hats. She watched a girl of student age with brick-red hair and yellow earmuffs step elegantly off her still-coasting cycle even as she guided it into place in a crowded bike stand, as a swan or a duck folds its wings as it lands on water, instantly adapting itself to its new element.

She enjoyed, too, the comedy of the buildings, strung together like chains of paper dolls, with their plain flat facades and intricate cut-away gables. She liked how they squeezed together, shiggling up along each stretch of canalside land like cartoon birds on a tree branch, to always let one more in.

The conference was being held in the university, situated just where the canals, on her phone's map, began their strange geometric ripples out towards the suburbs, giving the city the look of a theatre seating plan on a booking website. The university buildings were of grey stone, made more solid by the proximity of so much water. Inside, the corridors were busy with the bright traffic of education, the intent loitering of university students bent upon their sure intellectual nourishment, and the busyness grew the further she walked, not stopping when she reached the rooms forming the conference suite.

The large reception area was half-full, but beginning to empty, as people followed the sound of their own voices through a series of doors at the rear into the room that presumably held the welcome address. On one side were rows of tables set up for registration. On the other, full-height windows giving onto an internal courtyard with statues and low box hedges. There were poster-banners hanging on the walls, and information boards. Some of the banners had photos of Leonard on them, blown up. They made her smile. A giant of the field, she was going to call him. Whatever happened, she would have to steal some time to go back to the hotel and finish the speech.

Leonard's friend Deborah was overseeing one of the reception tables. She called Jenny over, jumping her over what remained of the queue, and gave her a name badge, some meal tickets for the cafeteria, and a tote bag containing, it transpired, two journal copies, the conference programme, some Dutch chocolate, a supposedly hi-tech new kind of phone case, and a USB stick and decent-looking metal water bottle carrying sponsor logos.

She stowed the badge in her handbag and followed the stragglers into the auditorium.

The room was larger than she had expected, and fuller. She guessed over three hundred people, maybe closer to four. All for Leonard, in part at least. She made her way down the near-side aisle until she found a row with an unoccupied end seat. She sat, and took a notebook and pen from her bag. From the tote, the glossy programme.

Frankie was already at the podium, mousing away at the computer, and there was Leonard, in the front row, turned in his seat to face the auditorium, fielding the occasional shouted greeting and responding with awkward waves of his arm. He wore an expression of genial bemusement, like someone waiting outside a surprise party that was no surprise at all. He'd be looking on the conference with a mixture of pleasure and dismay, Jenny presumed, for who would wish such a thing upon themselves?

In the audience, Jenny saw faces she recognised: faces she could put not just names to, but job titles, paper titles, journals and books, and scandals and fallings-out and endless dwindling shreds of gossip. Everyone was here. A few people waved, hesitantly, in her direction, and she gave little waves back. She had been away so long, she had no idea if she still belonged here, amongst these people. The return of the prodigal linguist. Last year this conference had been in Atlanta, and she'd not even gone. Now, thanks to Leonard – thanks to Frankie – she was closing the show, a star turn, and doubtless trailing shreds of gossip herself.

She turned to face the front, fixed her eyes on the screen behind the stage, and gave herself over to the timeless time of conferences, that particular form of it that extends spatially, like a desert, or the narrative of a dream, that goes on without duration, and has no limit until it is done. Whatever was going to happen, it would not happen in here. For now, at least, she was safe.

Eventually, Frankie looked to Leonard, checked her watch, and walked from the podium to centre-stage. People quietened, the doors into the auditorium were closed, and Frankie took up a pose that Jenny recognised from her most private, painful dreams. Frankie was about to launch herself upon them. Jenny tensed herself to listen.

Frankie Gerrity was her dearest friend, still; her lover and partner for three-and-a-half crucial, bitter years – years that had expanded in the rear-view mirror until they seemed now to hold within them most of her significant life, especially now that they existed on the far side of another all-consuming relationship: the marriage to a man that had seemed to her at the time a definitive turning-over of her life, a gleeful flight across a burning bridge. She didn't think that now. But equally she didn't know how to think herself back to the person she had been before.

Frankie had been ten years older than Jenny when they had first met, and Jenny supposed she still was; although a year, and a decade, carry a different charge and weight as you age. Jenny was now adrift from forty, turning hopelessly in the current, while Frankie seemed to carry fifty-three like a mark of distinction, like it was something glorious and impractical she wore for formal occasions, but would shrug off and leave, carefully folded, in the cloakroom the moment she was able.

'Welcome, welcome, welcome,' Frankie said, spreading her arms.

Jenny couldn't bear to listen, any more than she could bear to hear her own voice on a recording.

Frankie walked the stage in her jacket and trousers and squeaky purple shoes, introducing a skip into her step now and then as she talked. She was wearing a headset microphone, like a pop star or a motivational speaker. Her hands were always on the go. She touched at her lip, put a hand to her ear, then rested it on a hip – or a haunch, as she would no doubt have it. But she was good, god she was good. Her introduction was witty, considered, complimentary to the University of Amsterdam, Amsterdam itself, the guests, the food, the weather. But this was a preamble, Jenny could tell. Frankie was building to something. Her voice slowed, and she stood still, as if to consider how best to proceed.

'But we are here for another reason, too,' she said. 'This is no ordinary meeting of the International Society for

Philology and Linguistics. We are also here to celebrate the life and career of one among us who has, I think, influenced and inspired and helped more people in this room, directly or indirectly, than anyone else in his intellectual field, in our time. I'm talking about Leonard Peters, whose –'

Her words were interrupted by an abrupt surge of applause, with yelps and yells and here-heres thrown in for good measure. Jenny, startled, saw how her own, rather polite hand-clapping was out of step with the wave of approbation filling the room. It went on and on. Someone yelled out Leonard's name. There was even a whistle. And then laughter. The woman in the next seat, Jenny saw, was holding her hands up to clap right in front of her face, and was biting her lip. She looked like she was about to cry. Jenny looked back at Frankie, and saw that Frankie was looking at Leonard, her head on one side, watching to see how he would react to this extraordinary, unprecedented uprush of feeling. Leonard, Jenny saw, was staring back at Frankie, holding her gaze. Jenny looked from one to the other, confused until, after maybe a minute of this, Frankie motioned to the audience to quieten down, but genially, ironically, acknowledging the appropriateness of the gesture.

'Phew,' she said. 'Well. You're all correct, of course.' She clapped, herself. 'Leonard. What can we say about Leonard Peters? There are people here who remember Leonard when wearing a beard was a political statement.' She clicked her remote and a picture of him appeared on the huge screen behind her, from before Jenny had known him. He was in a turtleneck sweater and a wide-lapelled jacket. 'A time when men still cut themselves shaving and stuck cotton wool on the cuts, and you could buy typewriter ribbons, and computer mice had hard little rubber balls inside of them that you had to take out and clean, like real mice.'

Jenny had her pen in her hand, but though she listened, she wrote nothing down. Her main thought had been that she wanted to be sure she didn't repeat tomorrow anything Frankie said today, but really she was aghast at her friend's facility with words, her sense of being at home on the stage. It was appalling, really. It was scarcely to be borne.

Partly Frankie focused on Leonard, and partly she did the simple job of laying out the content and scope of the conference to come. She picked out people in the audience as they cropped up in her narrative, and made them stand and turn and wave to the rest of the room. She outlined themes, dropped names, suggested awkward and amusing questions for particular panels. Jenny realised she was going to name her, too, and then there it was:

'Jenny Thursley, of course, many of you will know, in particular for her instrumental championship and promulgation of Leonard's ideas both here and abroad – and in fact her insightful and often unexpected extension and redirection of them. We are particularly honoured to have her here, all the way from the University of California, Berkeley, to give the closing address to what is undoubtedly a historic, and is likely to be a highly emotional, conference.'

Jenny barely heard her, however, for the ringing of blood in her ears, and the strain it took to stand and turn and smile in acknowledgement, for she could hardly dip her head in shame, could she? But it was quickly over, and she was able to sit, and concentrate again on Frankie.

'If Leonard is to be remembered in conferences to come,' she was saying, 'if such things continue to exist, in this benighted world, then it should be for this: that he, as good as singlehandedly, revived the term philologist. For as long as I can remember, youngster that I am, for as long as I have known that there were words for words – that words, in other words, were also things – we have been in thrall to the linguists, and the structuralists. We have been under their thumbs, their *paradigmatic* thumbs, beholden to their love of the deep currents that flow beneath the surface of the ocean of language.

'But, the deeper you dive, the colder it gets, and the darker the water, and the weirder, frankly, the fish. I name no names. You know who you are. So, is it childish to want to splash and swim about in the warm upper layers of language? Very well, it is childish. Yet that is where we swim, we philologists.

'We may be building castles on sand – that's what the structuralists would say, or even on air, on a structure that rests its foundations on nothing, as the word is attached to its sense by no rational relation. We are – or we have been taught to think we are – like Wile E. Coyote, as he runs off the edge of the cliff.'

She clicked the remote, and the cartoon animal appeared in a clip on the screen, doing just that. It – he – ran off the cliff, heading out straight into the air, then looked down, then out at the viewer, his face a frozen explosion of panic. Before he could fall, Frankie clicked the remote again, and stopped the clip. She stood facing the screen, as if in contemplation of his fate. She stood there for a full thirty seconds before she spoke again.

'Like him,' she said, 'in his brief moments of airborne triumph, we are free' – she turned back to address the audience – 'and we will use our brief moments to build. For that inventive desert predator, it is a matter of seconds before he is reclaimed, recuperated, by the logic of gravity. For us, from the first Mesopotamian scratchings to the present day, it is a few millennia. The scale is different, but the function is the same.

'For we are all building castles on the abyss, but while we may build, and until some theorist comes along to point out that we are building on nothing, that there is no ground, no final source of meaning to authenticate the entire process – our habit, egregious, unforgivable and *naive* as it is, of making up names and giving them to things, and our making music from those names – for an arbitrary relationship, like an arbitrary structure, like a snowflake or an ice crystal, can have a beauty of its own – then why shouldn't we build? And why shouldn't what we build be beautiful? And why shouldn't we take the time to take pleasure in looking back at what we and others before us have built, and marvel at its beauty?'

She stopped speaking, and drooped, playful, like a ballerina wrung clean of energy. Applause warped the room, and shouts. It was, after all, quite a performance. Frankie pulled herself back up, and put her hand to her chest. Jenny found that her own smile had widened into a grin, and that her eyes, too, were set ready to cry.

'So it is fitting that we are here in great city of Amsterdam,' Frankie said, when she had got her breath back, 'where flourished what the Dutch call, and you will forgive me, De Gouden Eeuw. The Golden Age. In French, L'Age d'Or.' She said it again, throwing out a hand like an opera singer and yawing the vowels, making them a parody:

'L'Aaage d'Oorrr.

'The very idea of this l'Age d'Or, this Golden Age,' she went on, 'people will tell you, is a misnomer. Nothing was ever that great, ever that golden. But I see it the other way around. It is the act of looking, the act of wanting, that is golden, that confers the lustre we find there, where we look.' She was back on Jenny's side of the stage, and Jenny felt sure that, though Frankie wasn't looking in her direction, some part of what she was saying was for her ears. 'We paint particular moments in the past as glorious, or innocent, or good, because it is a means of anchoring ourselves, of tying ourselves into our history. So let's do that now. Let's anchor ourselves in the history of language, and plant a flag for future generations, who will look back and say – and I think they're right – that this was a Golden Age for philology.

'With which thought, I take great pleasure in welcoming you to the forty-fifth Conference of the International Society of Philology and Linguistics. Dank je wel, en welkom.'

There was more applause, but Jenny was first up the aisle and out of the room into the foyer and at the refreshment table, with its coffee cups, serried in ranks like extras in a Leni Riefenstahl film. The servers fussed with one of the great Dalek-like coffee flasks, while people started to gather either side of her.

'Jenny?'

She turned. It was, she thought, Andrea Owen. Was that it? Verb conjugation in the romance languages, something like that.

'Andrea, right?'

'Yes. Good to see you.'

'And you.'

'It's been ages, hasn't it?'

Jenny took a cup of coffee, and nodded.

'And you're doing the plenary, tomorrow.'

She nodded again, and as she did they locked eyes. Andrea Owen widened her gaze and lifted the corners of her mouth in a smile that had fled almost before it was there. 'I just don't know. I really don't,' she said, shaking her head.

Jenny nodded brightly in confusion, and muttered something indistinct even to herself as she backed away from the table, taking her leave in a vague amenable way from Andrea Owen, letting incomers drift in between them until their line of communication became severed.

She drank greedily from the coffee cup, enjoying the scald of the liquid on her palate, then went over to the reception tables and asked the woman there where she could smoke. The woman suggested the little outside courtyard, but that was too close by. There were already people there.

Somewhere further? She followed the directions down a dogleg corridor until she found a door that took her outside to another, smaller courtyard. Courtyard was too grand a word. It was like the bottom of a light well, though no sunlight reached down here. Poured concrete walls on three sides, a grey metal service entrance, a big four-wheeled industrial bin. Up high, thick skeins of cables ran along the walls and around the corner; a single horizontal wire trailed from it a creeper of some kind. She took her cigarettes and lighter from her bag. It was cold with no sun on her, and she'd left her coat in the auditorium.

Since moving to the US she was down to one cigarette a day, more or less, in honour of her adopted homeland. She smoked more at conferences and the like. It was so much more useful a vice now that fewer people did it.

She had been there no more than a minute, and had barely taken that first deep, and deeply freighted drag, when the door opened, bringing a person through it. Male, roughly her age, clearly from the conference.

'Hi there,' he said. 'Jennifer? Mind if I join you?'

She was holding her cigarette arm upright, its elbow cupped in the hand of her other arm, which she held across her body against the cold. The voice, and the face, were Dutch. She tried to think who it might be, if it was someone she knew. She waved the tip of the cigarette in as tight an ellipse as she could manage without seeming rude.

'I'm Jaap Vos,' he said, and held out his hand.

It took a second for the name to click.

'Jaap, of course. Forgive me.' She smiled, and swapped her cigarette to her left hand so as to be able to take his.

'I was hoping to have seen you at the dinner last night.'

They dropped hands, and he took out a cigarette and tamped it on the back of his wrist, then put it in his mouth.

'I wasn't able to be there,' she replied. 'Apologies. I only just flew in. Things have been rather hectic.'

He shrugged, cigarette bobbing, then lit up.

'Well,' he said. 'It's good to meet you finally, at least. I'm thrilled you're here. I consider it an honour.'

This, then, was Jaap, the leading light of the University of Amsterdam, who'd been behind bringing the international conference to the city for the first time. They'd corresponded, perhaps no more than three or four emails each way, over the past year or eighteen months – but long ones, interesting ones. He got what she'd been doing, that was certain, and she remembered how pleasing those emails had been to receive, how intrigued she had been at the idea of meeting the person who sent them – and then how she had contrived to put them, and him, out of her mind.

'I've been very much pushing you on my PhDs. I don't know if you saw, in my last mail...' Then, when he saw her response. 'No, don't worry.'

'I feel awful.'

'No, really. Don't worry. Perhaps I can introduce you to one or two of them, if we get the chance.'

'Yes, of course. Anyway it seems like it's all going to be a great success,' she said, nodding towards the door.

'Well, it's an important moment. Important to get it right, you know, for Leonard.'

'Absolutely.'

In his style Jaap Vos was eminently Dutch: the faded black needlepoint cords and politely off-beam jacket, with a scarf pulled in an elegant sideways knot at the throat. His slicked-back hair had streaks of grey winding through it, the hair thick enough to swallow them whole and spit them out again behind the ears. He was unabashedly handsome, with a touch of prettiness about the nose and lips, though the skin was beginning to loosen and pouch. Men could get away with not colouring their hair, just as they could get away with turning up to conferences in a good jacket that found its goodness in its decades of use, rather than in its newness. Men never said 'this old thing', she thought, because every bloody thing they wore was this old thing. She half-listened as he went on about the university, his department, the doctoral students of his who would be presenting at the conference.

He had smoked quicker than her, however, and now he

brushed the lit end of his cigarette down the wall to put it out. The tip dislodged and fell to the ground where it glowed, iridescent, like a dead insect. He put his shoe over it.

'If Leonard could see me now. Shit,' he said

He shook his head, but her incomprehension must have shown. He gestured with the butt in his hand. 'Leonard,' he said.

'Leonard.'

'You know, Leonard.'

The point at which he was going to have to tell her was also the point at which he no longer had to.

So much that is spoken in life is redundant. Verbal communication as an overlapping and repetitive series of superfluities. A call to prayer with no prayer to call to. White noise, chatter, birdsong. A doily all cutwork and no mat.

Leonard had lung cancer.

Jaap tried to say something, to recover the moment, but it was no good. Barely thinking, for fear of what she might think, Jenny ditched her cigarette, hitched her bag on her shoulder and walked through the door he held open for her. He talked as they went, keeping step behind her even when she increased her pace, but she didn't answer. Did not look left. Did not look right. What point looking, when the faculty of sight had so evidently left her?

Leonard had lung cancer and he was dying of it. Everybody knew.

She said nothing.

How could she not know? How did he... how could that be?

There was nothing to say.

It was far gone, Jaap was telling her, beyond all beyonds,

and everybody knew. He was dying, dead, as good as dead. The fact that everybody knew was clear from his shock at the fact that she didn't. Everyone in the lecture theatre. All her former friends and colleagues, the professors and professors emeritus that had flown in to pay their respects: they all knew. The early career academics from Utrecht and Berlin: they knew. The grad students from the department here in Amsterdam: them, too. Everybody but her.

She thought of how he'd been that morning, in the breakfast room. The three of them, stood at the table. How clear it was, now. Even the way Frankie had taken her hand spoke of it, her smile, her gentle reticence.

At the entrance to the conference foyer, which was still buzzing with coffee break chatter, she stopped and turned to face him.

'Look,' she said. 'I need to use the toilets.'

He was talking on and on, his demeanour full of understanding, but she refused to listen. There were people milling about, talking, laughing, finishing their coffees. Some of them were starting to drift towards one or other of the first panel events. They all knew. Servers were collecting up coffee cups. *They* probably knew. The depth of her ignorance was staggering, dumbfounding even. There was no sign of Leonard, thank god. She would have to speak to him. The thought of it made her feel faint with nausea. She would have to. But how *could* she? What could she say? She felt exposed, ridiculous, standing there with Jaap, him talking, her oblivious, the idiot from America. There were some people from the conference crowd looking at them, where they stood. Perhaps they did present something of a tableau.

She cut across what Jaap was saying, spilling or spewing

some words or other, she didn't know what. Yes, she was fine; he shouldn't worry; no doubt they would see each other later. She took her phone from her bag and thumbed it on. She wasn't even sure what she wanted with it, the stupid thing. She stood there, looking off back down the corridor, the way they'd come. Leonard was dead.

Behind her, she heard Jaap laugh.

A soft sound, not unkind, as if to himself.

'Sorry,' he said, when she turned to face him, for she was not ready to be laughed at, not just now. He threw his hand out, a weak conciliatory gesture, that seemed to want to draw on some meaning that was latent in the air between them.

'Sorry, it's a stupid thing,' he said.

She said nothing.

'It's just... I've just realised what it is you remind me of. I was trying to think, and seeing you standing there like that, I've got it.'

She shrugged. She had no interest in reminding him of someone else.

'Sorry. I'll explain later.'

Later, she thought. What's later?

The last people had gone into the events. She turned without saying anything more and went to the ladies, where she sat in a stall and put her face in her hands and didn't cry. She thought she might, but she didn't. She took out the conference programme from her bag and flicked through it, looking for some hint, some confirmation, but how would there be? How would you possibly include that information in something like this? As she turned the pages she came upon her name, the final slot tomorrow afternoon. Nothing is settled, she read. Contingency and desire. What trash!

How could you trust words to do anything, when every sentence contained eight trapdoors to send you plummeting like that fool coyote into humiliating meaninglessness?

And how on earth was she supposed to give her speech tomorrow, what there was of it, now? No one has done more than him. Leonard has cancer. A giant in the field. Leonard is dying. I have the honour. The man is as good as dead.

When she was sure she wasn't going to be sick, she washed her hands then set off back towards the conference, but couldn't bring herself to go in. An attendant asked her if she was alright.

'I just need a moment,' she said. 'Thank you. I'll get some air, I think.'

'The way to the outside square is here, if you like,' the woman said, and gestured towards the inner courtyard next to the foyer.

'Thank you.'

'You're welcome.'

She went back out into the cold air. The courtyard had something of the feel of a cloister about it, its low, close-clipped hedges running in patterns across the gravel and paving stones, forming a rudimentary maze. Placed here and there between them were taller ornamental shrubs, four of them, and four abstract sculptures, stood like wanderers in the maze, that had become lost, despite its obvious simplicity, and the lowness of the walls. Jenny sat on a stone bench. She put her hands under her legs and felt the deep cold of the stone, how it went all the way through. She would give herself ten minutes, then go back in. A giant in his field, she thought. I have the great honour.

4

Lieve had her notebook out on the long desk-type shelf that ran the length of the back of the row of seats in front. Every time she sat in one of the lecture halls she wondered if there was a word for this kind of shelf in English. There wasn't one that she knew of in Dutch, Flemish or French. It reminded her of the shelf that ran along the back of the pews in the church at home, in the village where she grew up.

Her pen hovered over the page. She always filled up pages and pages at these things, but usually with stuff entirely unconnected to what was actually being said. Random thoughts, fragments, whatever came into her head. Lectures, like church services, like theatre, were a good stimulus to thought, no matter what the person at the front thought they were imparting. This particular paper was nothing special. She woke her phone and tweeted, in English: Listening to Klara Brouwer: multiethnolects in second-generation immigrant populations in Germany @UvA_Amsterdam #ISPLConf – fascinating stuff! Then she switched apps and messaged Mysha.

You here yet?

Yes, came the reply. I'm behind you, six rows back.

Lieve turned slowly to look. There she was. She had gone with the leather jacket. She gave a discreet wave, and her phone buzzed on the shelf. She had set it to silent but forgotten to turn off vibrate. The woman next to her gave her a quick glance of disapproval.

The message read: So... all set, followed by three emojis. A woman student in a mortar board, the dancing couple again, and then a purple evil-looking smiley face with horns.

Lieve lifted her hands in a dumbshow of frustration, placed them over her eyes, and let her head fall forward to bounce in front of her. No, no, no, she thought. Don't be an idiot. She removed her hands, only to find she was being side-eyed again by her neighbour. She gave a simper of apology, turned her phone face-down on the shelf, and took up her pen.

The crazy thing about social media, she wrote, in Dutch, is that it allows you to apply a critique to your life in real time.

She looked up at Klara Brouwer, observed her for a moment, then back down at the page. If she looked up every now and then, people would assume she was taking notes on the paper.

Compare to the traditional bedtime diary. Like that, it thrives on gossip, on the microscopic acts of social grace: flirtation, resentment, jealousy, but crucially it allows you to reflect on these acts even as you experience them. Fleeting emotional states freeze-framed, magnified, rotated in three dimensions like a virtual model on-screen, commented on, broadcast. Interior life as shared doc. Combination of immediacy and critical distance means you live life like a teenager again. What must it be like for actual teens? So many lives lived at full speed. Speed without direction. How does it affect your decision-making? Does it even make things worse? Encourage you to make bad choices for the sake of dissecting them straight afterwards?

She looked over to where Jaap was sitting, on the other side of the auditorium, a row forward from her. He had positioned himself in that elegantly contorted way he had, with his legs sticking out into the aisle, but his body turned back this way. His head was tilted at an angle equally intelligent and painful, as if the discomfort of his pose guaranteed the degree of his attention.

She wrote: Men deal so well with age. Confidence comes from patriarchy, sure, of course, but isn't it the social structures that grow out of the biological situation, even though that's what civilisation's meant to save us from.

She quickly looked at the woman next to her, then leaned over her notebook, shielding the page with her arm. She worried what she was writing might be nonsense, but you had to keep going, didn't you?

M wrong about JV, she wrote. His intrinsic sense of self is protected by the social structure in which he is embedded. He can be a man and a lecturer all at the same time. The two roles can coexist, overlap, remain ambiguous and indistinct. When he looks at you there is something retained. Most men (boys) unable to control impulses even in looking. You can tell what a man is thinking simply by seeing what he is looking at. Men walking down the street.

She crossed out this last line, and went on.

A man in his forties/fifties/sixties? has tactics, and strategy, but it's only then, in middle age, that they acquire it. It's only then that they need it. Women need it much earlier, right from the start. You pick it up when you're still a teenager, when the boys are idiots pure and simple. Men use their intelligence tactically, like women use make-up, hair, clothes. Intellect as clothing? She paused and sucked on the end of her pen.

Then a series of increasingly scrawled notes: Intellect as style, beyond fashion. Easier change clothes than mind. Grow out of clothes, wear them out. Not same with ideas. Nobody throws out their intellectual wardrobe. You wear as an adult the same set of ideas you did as a child. Fundamental beliefs = underwear? Hygiene. Support.

For e.g. the woman with JV after coffee break. Late thirties/early forties. Grey dress, long black boots. Long hair worn up. In that strange stage of life where women disappear either into career or home. Him talking, her just standing there, whatever he was trying on with her had no chance of working. You could see it in the way they were standing. But still it is he that I have the connection to. None possible between me and her. None of the chains of influence and confluence I feel with a man of that age. Not just sex. I could reach a hand out to him and he could pull me up to where he is, but her, whoever she is? I don't think so. It should be that I am learning from her/people/women like her.

Leonard Peters thanked the first speaker, then began the introduction for the second. People coughed and shifted in their seats, and Lieve took the opportunity to turn and quickly scan the room, running a hand self-consciously over her head as she did so.

There she was, in fact, sitting in the row behind Mysha. The woman who'd been talking with Jaap. She must have come in late. Lieve looked again at Jaap, then back at the woman. Lieve's hand rested on her head, then dropped to her ear, and she fiddled with her upper helix ring. There was something about their positioning in the room, where she'd chosen to sit in relation to him, that was not random, but offered no easy explanation. Some form of triangulation she couldn't yet quantify.

Jenny had been intending to sit in on a panel discussion chaired by her former colleague Derek Bentner in the main lecture theatre, but instead she took herself to listen to the smaller panel that Leonard was chairing. So like him, to rock up to his own Festschrift, the pinnacle of his career, a lovingly constructed peak from which he could survey the forest that had sprung up around the globe, all grown from seeds carried on the four winds from his originating tree, and instead of listening to people sound off grandly about how important it all was, he'd chosen to head up a panel of PhD students from Bupkis, Ohio, or Dubrovnik, or wherever, who were actually taking his ideas and doing something with them. Not leaving them in any decent state in the process, you'd have to assume, but that was Leonard for you. And PhD students.

She'd slunk into the back row near the end of the first paper to sit with the other no-goodniks, noting with annoyance that Jaap Vos had picked the same session to attend. She had the conference programme out on the shelf in front of her and a hand pressed to her forehead, making a visor for her eyes. She slipped a pill of chewing gum into her mouth, fervently wishing it were cyanide.

Leonard was the very model of professional ease. He had his watch off, laid on the table in front of him in that classic visual trope of academia. The first panellist had just finished his presentation, and the ease and generosity with which Leonard fielded questions and steered the conversation, while making gentle but incisive points of his own, she would have found disarming, if she hadn't already been comprehensively disarmed, dismembered, irradiated.

The second presenter took to the podium. She was visibly shaking with nerves. The sheaf of papers in her hands, as she faced the room, was in constant, delicate motion. Mid-twenties, well turned out in a skirt suit and ballet flats, she could have been Jenny herself twenty years ago: she had thrown up in the loos ten minutes before her first conference paper. It was for her the taste of academia, to this day: the acid bite of reflux.

The girl spoke in Dutch, with an English translation appearing slide by slide on the screen behind her, but Jenny ignored that and concentrated on the speaking woman, fascinated by her uncertain delivery, and pleased not to be able to follow what she was saying. She had always found it soothing to listen to people speak in languages she didn't understand, and though more or less parsable on the page, Jenny found the Dutch language in its spoken iteration delightfully, incorrigibly alien, the way it twisted familiar phonetic tics into gnarly thickets of incomprehension.

It took a few minutes, and a few clicks of the mouse to change slides on the screen, before Jenny realised the presenter wasn't shaking from nerves. She had a condition, multiple sclerosis or some such. She watched her more compassionately, but with reduced interest. Then she stopped watching her, and watched Leonard instead. What she was looking for, she didn't know.

She did know, of course. She was looking for the mark of death.

Such a thing must exist, she thought. In the realm of the cancerous, at least. She had had an aunt who had died of cancer of the stomach, and you could see it in her from half a mile away. Even a teenager could see it. Her aunt, too, was prone to vomiting, the confused response of the body to something inside it that it wanted to get outside, and that it thought it could simply wash out with the rest of the garbage. On Leonard, though, she thought, as she observed him and he in turn watched the woman talk to the room, on him there was no mark, or nothing that she could distinguish from the general marks of age, which were nothing more than death smudging you with its thumb, smearing your features, letting you know you're not forgotten, you haven't been passed over.

After a while, she got her laptop out and set it on her lap, then opened up the file containing her speech, what she had of it. She scrolled through the text, scanning for some place of purchase, somewhere she might step into it. The research itself was fine: how the subjunctive functioned in different European languages so as to let you bring what might or might not be to bear on what explicitly *is*. The bits of biography she had managed to incorporate, on the flight, were mostly bearable, in themselves. It was everything else that was wrong: the words, the tone, the gaps around and between the words, where people would see her for what she was. The whole thing was written from a position of fatal naivety. She skimmed back up to the top and re-read the opening, mouthing the words to herself while the panel went on around her, applause and the sound of knocking on the wood of the shelves. It would have to go, she thought. It would all have to go.

While the final presenter was taking questions, Jenny slipped out into the foyer and found a spot over by the tall glass windows by the courtyard to wait for Frankie, who had presumably been in another session. People began to arrive, from all directions. They came in clumps and clusters, and as these met the other groups they mingled and merged, people kissing cheeks and shaking hands, nodding their heads and calling names and laughing, looking around for other people to bring into their little cliques. There was something ferocious about the process. Some people waved to Jenny, and she waved back, vaguely, not making it an invitation, indicating her watch if someone seemed to be about to come over.

When Frankie came in from the main auditorium, it was in her own little grouping. Jenny raised her hand, held it still for a moment, then beckoned. She had always known how to make herself, discreetly, seen, to Frankie at least. It seemed the trick, if trick it was, still worked. Frankie paused in what she was saying, then extricated herself from the group and drifted as if at random in Jenny's direction.

'Hello again, darling,' she said, and squeezed Jenny's arm.

Jenny didn't respond, but simply opened her eyes wide, a dumbshow of helplessness.

'What's the matter?' her friend said. 'What's wrong?'

Leonard was in the foyer now, too, talking with one of the presenters from his panel. Frankie followed her gaze.

'Yes?' she said, uncertain. Then: 'What?'

Then, finally, she let her face and then her shoulders drop. 'No? What? Leonard? Don't tell me you didn't know.'

'Why didn't you tell me?' Jenny said. Her voice was a rasp, all sound hollowed out. She cleared her throat, and said it again. 'Why didn't you tell me?'

'I just assumed. I mean, everyone knew. It wasn't exactly a secret.' Then, seeing Jenny's reaction, 'Bloody hell, sorry.' She lowered the pitch of her voice. Her hand on Jenny's arm again, the squeeze this time feeling through the fabric for the flesh underneath. 'Stupid, stupid me. Look, do you want to come and get lunch now.' She gestured with her head towards Leonard, over the other side of the room.

Jenny could barely even shake her head. It just jerked from side to side, like a broken toy.

'No, I suppose not. Let's get out of here. Come for lunch.'

'I'm not sure I can face lunch, if I'm honest.'

'Well, don't eat anything, then. But you will talk to him, properly, right? At some point?'

'Yes. Of course.'

'Come on then. Wait over there. I just need to check he's sorted for lunch and everything.'

Within minutes they had their coats and were out of the university and back in the cold bright heart of the city. Frankie had a great big faux fur hat, Jenny nothing but her coat and gloves, but in a way the cold was a comfort.

Frankie had Jenny's arm in hers, but they had not spoken. The streets seemed intent on presenting themselves as immediately, uncomplicatedly hospitable. The lines of light scribbled on the water. The houses. A boat puttered towards them, carrying a few happy, cosseted tourists. Dogs being walked, trotting with purpose. Ahead of them on the road a small flatbed truck was parked. It had hoisted an extending ladder up to an open window and up this was moving a square platform the size of a modest kitchen table, motorised somehow, carrying an empty bookcase, laid on its back and strapped in place.

Cyclists passed them, in both directions. Jenny marvelled again at the poise of the people riding them. They sat so upright, and seemed to expend so little energy in getting themselves about. This one, coming towards them, had a great scooped wooden bucket fixed to the front of their bicycle, carrying two small children wrapped up in padded jackets, like baby pelicans in the pouched beak of their mother. Their eyes, as they went by, rested uncritically on her. One day, Jenny thought, those children would themselves cycle these same streets with kids of their own sat in wedge-shaped wooden troughs – it seemed inevitable. They walked on. In through a basement window, someone was working at a laptop, a cup of tea beside her on the desk, a series of little pots and painted wooden toys lined up on the window sill. She didn't look up as they went by.

'Bloody hell,' said Jenny. 'It's sickening. Everything just works.' They came to a side road, and a car paused to let them cross over. She gestured at the driver, almost in irritation. 'See what I mean?' In the distance a tram went over a bridge, with its escort of bicycles. 'Why can't other countries be like this? Why don't we all just move here?'

Frankie didn't answer. Instead, she said, 'This'll do.' She indicated a restaurant sign sticking out over the street some fifty yards ahead. 'You'll eat a pancake, won't you?'

'Oh, come on.'

'No, you come on. I'm having a pancake. You can eat what you like.'

Jenny did feel the lack of something. Her head was fizzing with tiredness, and her body felt as if it stood on the edge of a precipice. Food might offer something, fuel or solace. Or distraction, at least.

The restaurant was half full, with red and white checked tablecloths and clunky wooden chairs. When they had ordered, the two women looked at each other. Frankie's look was one of blunt assessment. Jenny wrinkled her nose in response. She didn't know whether she was trying to be cute, or if she was about to start crying. She didn't know where to begin, because she didn't know where she wanted to end up.

Frankie placed her hand on the table, next to her cutlery setting. Jenny regarded it. It was like an opening bid at bridge. A bid to which she had no reply.

'You're seriously telling me you didn't know,' Frankie said.

'I bloody well am. I'm fuming.' The words, once out of her mouth, had the stink of stupidity about them. She didn't know how serious she was supposed to be being.

'You're not fuming. You're distraught.'

'Whatever, I'm distraught. Next you'll be telling me I'm in shock.' She looked up at Frankie. 'Don't you dare tell me I'm in shock.' She pushed at her own knife and fork, snug in their folded paper napkin, and they rotated on the laminated cloth.

Yes, it was lung cancer. Yes, it was very bad. Leonard wasn't expected to last the year, unless there was a miracle, and miracles weren't being predicted. Even the summer was looking a tough proposition, although no you wouldn't necessarily know it to look at him. But then he'd start coughing and that was it. A carpet bombing that laid minutes of life at a time to waste. There were times, Frankie said, when life just paused for him; he had absences, either from coughing, or from pain, or just from the strict self-awareness that illness forces upon you. And he wasn't exactly old. Just sixty-six. 'It's terrible,' she said.

Their drinks came. A coffee for Frankie, a mint tea for Jenny that was, quite literally, a large-handled glass, thick as a jam jar, with thick sprigs of mint stuck in water. She mashed at the mint with a long-handled spoon.

'When did you know?' she said. 'Did he tell you? I'm assuming everyone else in the world knows. This Dutch guy, Jaap, he knew.'

'Jaap Vos? He knows everything.' Frankie waved her hand, a dismissal. 'Well, he's been discreet, but like I say it wasn't exactly a secret. I suppose I've known for six, eight months. Everybody in the department knows. But, Jenny, listen.' She considered her words for a moment. 'You're the one who took yourself out the loop. Who stopped replying to emails, and phone calls. And letters. *Letters*, Jen. Which it was your right to do, of course, and nobody blames you for your choices. But this is what happens when you sever all lines of communication. It's not just the things you don't want to hear that you don't hear.'

Jenny looked past Frankie, down the length of the restaurant. She shook her head, but she was shaking it at herself.

'How did he tell you?' she said.

'Darling, he told me with words.'

Jenny stopped stirring her tea and looked at her friend, but Frankie ignored her and went on. 'I was in town and I popped in to talk about something, this conference most likely. Now then Frankie, he said. Don't get ahead of yourself, but I've got cancer. He didn't want sympathy. He was smoking, you must remember, Jenny Wren, back when the ads still had a handsome doctor in them saying how good they were for you.'

'Christ. Poor bastard.'

'Poor bastard indeed.'

'I mean, it hasn't really sunk in.'

'Of course it hasn't.'

'What am I going to say tomorrow? Shit, Frankie. Everything I've written... I might as well chuck it out. Your talk was *so* good, you're so *good* at that kind of stuff. I can't do it.'

'Jenny.'

'Frankie, I can't. I'll stand up there and open my mouth and nothing will come out.'

'Well, what have you got prepared?'

'Oh, some stuff. But it's not that. That can take care of itself. It's the other stuff.' She suddenly had another flash of him at the party, the sheer ridiculousness of him, reaching out to her, and closed her eyes. 'I don't know,' she said. 'I just don't know. What am I supposed to say? He taught me everything I know.'

'No, he didn't,' Frankie said kindly, but with emphasis. 'He taught you everything *he knew*.'

'Perhaps.' Jenny considered her mint tea. It was a nice thing to say, a generous thing. It was exactly the sort of thing Frankie was expert as saying. 'Look,' she said, and she, too, softened her tone of voice. 'Frankie. About Leonard.'

'Yes.'

'Did he ever... I mean, one time, years ago, when I'd just got my first job at Manchester, he made a pass at me. And I just wanted to know...'

'Shit. Oh Jenny, I'm sorry.'

Frankie sat back in her chair, hard, and it creaked.

'Don't worry. It was nothing. I mean, I dealt with it. I never told anyone, because I didn't think it was worth telling. I just wanted to know if you'd heard of him doing it to anyone else.'

'No, never.' Frankie shook her head, thought, then shook it again, more emphatically. 'The stupid fucking idiot.'

'That's kind of what I thought. I just wondered.'

'Of course.'

Say something, Jenny pleaded, in her head. Now is your chance to say something that will make all this alright. Say something loving to me, something to give me hope. It's only that that will give me the courage to do stand up tomorrow and speak.

But nothing more was forthcoming.

The waitress came with their food: a pancake each, wide, speckled and thin, except for where they bulged in the middle with good things hidden. The smells of bacon and melted cheese joined with those of the coffee and mint. Jenny felt again like she was ready to cry. But it wasn't Leonard, or not just Leonard. And not just Frankie, this close to her.

In her childhood her mother had always said grace before meals, and something like it, she felt, was called for now. She needed to find a way to be thankful for the bare, only fitfully luminous fact of her existence, if she was to be able to speak at all to Leonard, or say anything about him.

Perhaps the ritual brought the feeling along in its wake.

She watched as Frankie cut a thin segment of her pancake, folded it onto her fork with her knife and lifted it to her mouth. Frankie's eyes flicked to Jenny's boots, sticking out to the side of the small table. Was that a smile there, hidden among the chewing? Jenny kinked her legs out further, letting the leather catch and caress the light from the lamps. Frankie raised her eyebrows.

It was with Frankie that Jenny had first understood desire. This was what she told herself, but she had no idea if the truth survived each individual telling. She had loved and been in love before she knew Frankie. She had had boyfriends, of varying degrees of seriousness, and fierce loving attachments to a number of women, or girls as they mostly were at that stage. She had desired and lusted and keened and pashed; and she had experienced these things in reverse, from the other end, too, but she had always felt fooled by desire. Desire was a psychological mechanism for getting you to want something. It always eventually revealed itself as part of the capitalist schema. Once you got what you desired, desire was extinguished, its object rendered obsolete, and you found you desired something else.

This was boring and frustrating, but what was more boring and more frustrating was the strange condition that desire should meet with, and be met with, an equal desire; to desire and be desired and have both those desires requited. She had tried to get this to work, many times. In reality, however, one person's desire was extinguished quicker than the other's. You were got, and were thus no longer desired, while you went on desiring. Or the other way around.

It was Frankie who awoke in Jenny an understanding that desire can grow not towards its own extinction, but towards a plateau of happiness in which it dissipates, a glorious unresolved chord, endlessly sustained. Desire shared becomes joy, self-replenishing. Two people can be all things to each other, versatile, multivalent. Two things at once. Just as leather boots, they once decided, the two of them, are at once phallic and vaginal, erect and dominant in look, but also passive and enfolding, something you had to physically insert yourself into.

It was over ten years ago now that they had met, at a conference, in fact, but it was over a weekend in Brighton, where Frankie lived, a short time afterwards, that they had confirmed their mutual fascination. Frankie had a girlfriend somewhere in the background. 'She bet me twenty pounds I couldn't seduce you,' Frankie had said, in bed in Jenny's B&B, which made Jenny feel both cheap and respectable for the first time in her lesbian existence. When Frankie turned up in Manchester the following weekend, to whisk Jenny to a gay pub twenty minutes' walk from her house, that she never even knew existed, it was with that actual twenty-pound note, so she claimed, that she bought the first round. The girlfriend dropped out of the picture soon afterwards.

They stayed in the pub until closing, talking, as they'd stayed in bed back in that B&B in Brighton until check-out time the next morning. The time was filled end to end with talk. In the pub, they talked and drank, taking turns: one drinking, while the other talked. In bed it was the same. Kissing was wasteful, because it stopped both mouths, but sex and reading hung together in an erotic symbiosis that was as nourishing as it was self-sustaining. They took books to bed, and one read while the other made love to her – just like the people who read newspapers to the workers in a Cuban cigar factory, in Frankie's comparison. A virtuous circle of reading and fucking, each feeding on and feeding the other. They read Jeanette Winterson, Christina Rossetti, Maya Angelou, John Donne. Angela Carter, Virginia Woolf and Vita Sackville-West. It was the humorous and the lyrical and the outrageous they were after, something that tripped off the tongue and ravished the ears.

It wasn't a constant endeavour, this reading and fucking, but it was what she remembered most of those years. An hour in bed was the equivalent of an afternoon. A golden afternoon was a weekend. A weekend a week. Time slowed, and slurred, drew itself out until it achieved perfect stillness. She had never been more turned on than when making love to Frankie, while Frankie read to her; never been more engaged with an author than when she was reading to Frankie, propped up on pillows, and legs tucked or extended, and Frankie was making love to her, pushing her to the very limits of concentration, until her mouth dried, and the page whited out, and her mind with it, and the book fell, held loose in her hand, to flop over the edge of the bed.

Jenny drew the blade of her knife across the pancake. She was reddening about the ears, she could tell, and her neck was rigid with fatigue, the tendons as stiff as rods of steel in concrete pillars. The worst of it was that they were in public, as if Frankie had kept her out in the open on purpose. She wanted above all to be back in Frankie's flat in Hove, with the window ajar, and the summer warmth rolling in to keep them fixed to the bed. Frankie dusting the back of her hand over her hip, her tummy, her flank. Wriggling her fingers in through her hair to scratch at her scalp. Or not even in bed. To be there would be enough. The curtains moving in the inconstant breeze. The snatches of talk drifting in from the pavement outside, lurid and hilarious. Half an hour alone with her, in private, was all that she needed. To talk, and to see her talk be heard. Jenny forked the slice of pancake into her mouth.

'I've got the answer to your question, though,' Frankie said. She leaned across the table, her voice low.

Jenny was suspicious. 'What?' she said.

'Why we don't all just move here, when it's all so bloody perfect.'

Jenny tried not to show her disappointment. 'Why, then?'

'It's the language.'

'The language?'

'It's so pigging ugly. Listen.'

There was a table of four Hollanders along from them, and Jenny followed the sideways dart of her eyes to check them out. A man was speaking: youngish, bearded, his hair angled in slick spikes across his forehead. His voice had a slurred cadence, it kept guttering out into a grim expectorating sound, like sandpaper. A sound you would never use in English, except to clear your throat. She listened for it now, and it came, regularly, horribly. She thought of the woman, in the panel, who'd given her paper in Dutch. There'd been a prettiness and a hesitancy about her – perhaps she was from the south of the country, or even from Flemish Belgium – but this voice at the table next to them seemed to turn the mouth and throat into a militarised zone.

'So yes,' Frankie said. 'Everything works so well, the

bicycles, the trams, the bloody toilets.'

'God, yes. The toilets. I'd forgotten about them.'

'But here's the thing. The language. That's their secret weapon. Their impenetrable defence. It's closer to English than German is, grammatically, but listen to it. It's an abomination.'

They both looked up.

The waitress was standing at their table.

'Is everything OK?' she said, in flawless English.

Frankie's smile lit up her face.

'Wonderful, thank you. Dank je wel.'

'Sure thing.'

'It is, though, isn't it?' Frankie said, when the waitress had gone, and they'd stopped, silently, snickering. 'It's enough to make you stab your ears.'

'English used to sound like that, too,' said Jenny. 'Remember. Knight. Fight.' She said the words again – knight, fight – but growling the ends of them, feeling the phlegm form in her mouth.

'Yes, but we made the mistake of changing, adapting. And so it was that we took over the world. Am I wrong in thinking it clever of them, to insist on sounding so barbaric?'

She waved her fork in the air, for emphasis. Jenny imagined leaning across the table and stilling her. Being with Frankie, but having to restrict themselves to this trivia, she felt like a child in a fairy tale, walking around and around a hedge of thorns grown up to hide a castle, looking for the tunnel that would take her inside.

Frankie had been understanding at the end, when Jenny, in a fit of desperate elation, had broken things off. That she had fallen in love with a man was not, for Frankie, a personal betrayal, but it did bespeak a practical question. If all she wanted, she had said, was to go off and have a good old-fashioned fuck, for old times' sake, for the reasons of the body, then just say it. It was something she could understand.

But that wasn't what she'd wanted.

If Jenny had been comprehensively seduced by Frankie, then it was still a seduction they both stepped into together, eyes open – Frankie was never anything other than fair and reasonable. This other thing had been a coup de foudre, plain and simple, a vicious attraction that swept all other considerations off the table, if only to fuck on it. There was nothing to be done.

Jenny knew what her problem was. She had framed it often to herself. It was that she felt she could only believe in the story of her life as a narrative in which each chapter was bigger and better – higher in style and grander in scale – than the last. Her affair with Frankie had been bigger than any romantic relationship she had had before that, and so, for it to end, and to efface it, her marriage must be bigger still. When it turned out that this was not the case – that her marriage was smaller, and meaner, and more humiliating – her belief in this myth of personal progress sputtered and died, and she fled west to California. She hadn't had a relationship in the two years she'd been there. Not of any kind. Instead, she had poured herself into teaching. Into research, and into her students. Now, she felt, she was all poured out. There was nothing more to give. Or what there was left was so precious, so essential, that it could not be risked. Those years of their life together now seemed unsurpassable, entirely wonderful, hazed into perfection.

The question was, did she have the strength of character to put herself back in her friend's life? It was only Frankie that could answer that question, but the answer was to be feared. She wanted to be saved, as she always wanted to be saved, but she was afraid that Frankie, having stooped once to save her, would not do it again. She needed Frankie to put down her cutlery and look at her and hold her gaze, and for both of them to reach their hands out across the table, and for nothing to be said, as nothing needed to be.

Instead, they ate. The conversation, somehow, managed to back away from the precipice. Frankie talked more about Leonard, the progress of his disease. About the conference attendees. She asked Jenny about her lecture, tomorrow, and received an evasive, weakly humorous reply.

'I had about a thousand words done, but they'll all have to go, every one of them. I'm tempted to just get up on stage and wing it.'

Frankie duly raised her eyebrows. On stage, and in print, were the only place where Jenny had never winged it, not once.

She had never done a bungee jump, but she felt sure in herself that it would hold no fear for her. She was used to flinging herself off things, as much as she was used to flinging herself into things. But work was work.

Jenny's phone pinged, and she reached for it. It was a text:

Jennifer. Apologies for this text of the blue. I got your number from Deborah Mackenzie. Don't go to the first session this afternoon. I have something I want very much to show you. It will explain my stupidity this morning! Come to Café Konos on north corner of Keizersgracht and Nieuwe Spiegelstraat at 1pm? Jaap.

'What is it?'

Jennifer pulled a face and passed Frankie the phone.

Her friend held it off to the side and squinted at the screen.

'Well, he's a smooth operator,' she said.

She passed the phone back and put her head adroitly on one side.

'What?' said Jenny. 'You don't think I'm going to go, surely?'

'Why ever not? He's an interesting man.'

'If you say so. How well do you know him?'

'A little, from the conference. And yes, he's alright, so far as I know. I've not heard anything bad. But, really, given the choice between this and another panel on, I don't know, variant coding of idiomatic expressions, I know what I'd do.'

'Well, you're an incorrigible flirt.'

The lie sat in the air between them.

'OK, I'll go and meet him for a coffee.'

Frankie raised her hand to call for the bill, then looked at Jenny and nodded at the phone. 'Go on, then,' she said. Jenny felt like she was being palmed off, got rid of. Whatever Jaap Vos had to offer was hardly compensation. She replied to the text.

'It's really good to see you again, Jen,' Frankie said, when they were outside. 'You're looking really great.'

They hugged, a touch closer this time than that morning. Jenny widened her nostrils and breathed in deeply, hoping to take into herself something of Frankie's scent, some thread or spoor leading back to the past, but there was nothing, just the sterile residue of hotel soap and shampoo.

They unhooked themselves.

Jenny had Frankie's hand in her hers and she shook it,

lightly, refusing to let go, playing at a desperation that she felt was real. Frankie let her do this. Eventually she gently extricated herself.

'See you later.'

'Yes. See you later.'

She'd not gone ten paces before she heard her name. She turned back, ready to be smitten, ready for whatever Frankie might smite her with, ready to dissolve or die.

Frankie's expression hovered halfway between that of a wicked Italian cherub and that of a saint, or at least an abbess.

'Twenty pounds says you can't seduce him,' she said.

Jenny could find nothing to say to this. She twitched her mouth into a wincing smile, flicked her eyebrows and turned again to go. She tossed her hair and stepped out smartly into the path of an oncoming cyclist. The cyclist yelped out a warning, swerved to avoid her, and then peddled off, throwing back over her shoulder a no doubt withering and entirely justified kite's tail of invective.

5

They had just crossed the Herengracht, walking arm in arm like two good friends on a fun day out, when Mysha abruptly swung them round to face the window of the shop they happened to be passing. It was a kitchenware store, and they pretended to inspect the display. Spoons, spatulas and tongs hung in a rainbow of primary colours; notched cookie cutters came nested in vicious circles like miniature mantraps; mixers had bowls big enough to bake a child in. Mysha pointed things out and they oohed and aahed. There was chrome, plastic, rubber: it was like the parlour of a sex fetishist.

Lieve looked down the street and then back.

When she did, she caught Mysha watching her, reflected in the window.

'What is it?' Lieve said.

'Nothing.'

She looked miserable, or something angrily like it.

'No, not nothing. What?'

'Your comments on my paper. You think I'm an idiot.

You think it's a lot of crap.'

'Mysha, hey.' Lieve tried to sound indignant, but couldn't help letting some weariness creep in, too. It was not a new complaint. 'I said there were some very good ideas in there.'

'Crap. You don't think it's good enough.'

'I think it's fine. We're approaching things differently, is all. You don't need to compare them.'

'Compare what? Compare our papers? I'm not comparing anything. I didn't say anything about your work, which is brilliant, obviously. I'm saying that you think my work is crap, that I'm too stupid to be here.'

Relieved, Lieve gave Mysha's arm a tug. Their quarry had re-emerged from the shop he'd ducked into. For an exquisite and knife-sharp moment she imagined he might be turning back towards them, but he didn't. He carried on along the street. They waited a few seconds, then set off after him, unhurriedly – for Jaap Vos, who powered around the Linguistics department like it was a government ministry, papers flapping under his arm and students bobbing in his wake, was dawdling. He stopped to light a cigarette, leaning into a shopfront until it took. He walked on, smoking, and now and then checking his phone.

She couldn't quite believe they were doing this. It was not a normal activity, but then that was Mysha for you. This is just a weird thing I'm doing with my friend, she told herself. And indeed, Mysha was a good friend. She was good at being a friend. Friendliness, in fact, came off her like an animal stink. You wanted to get closer to her to test it, to taste it, see how far you could bear it. And she was young, and that was infectious, too, or you hoped it was. But mostly the fun was limited to mobile phone nonsense, and shopping trips where

Lieve tried on a few things and bought nothing, and going to clubs she wouldn't normally have known even existed and dancing till she dropped, and, at the outer limit, a few disastrous attempts to set her up on dates. Nothing doing. Mysha had no idea what went on inside Lieve's secret heart.

They followed their PhD supervisor over another canal. He was heading away from the centre. They walked in silence, and Lieve guessed that Mysha took the silence as confirmation of her accusation. Their arms were still linked, and as they walked their bodies, or their coats, came together and parted, over and over, a companionable kiss and remove, kiss and remove.

'If I think you're an idiot,' Lieve said, 'it's not because of your work.'

Mysha said nothing for a few steps, then said, 'Oh, come on, it's not like I'm going to do anything.'

Which only meant, Lieve felt sure, that she was.

At the next canal, Jaap turned to the left, and they lost sight of him. They increased their pace, making the corner just in time to see him go down some steps into a café. It was Café Konos, a smart hipster-looking place with a chalkboard sign and a couple of trestle tables outside. The two women consulted quickly, then crossed to the far side of the bridge. Here they were out of the sun, and it was colder, but then they were wearing a full complement of scarves, hats and sunglasses, in a probably vain attempt at disguise. In fact, they were so piled high with accessories that they most likely stood out a mile away.

They positioned themselves next to a school group of British teenagers. If they stood close enough, they might look like they belonged with them. Jaap came up out of the café with a drink and sat at one of the trestle tables. He hunched in his jacket and looked again at his phone.

'God, I need a coffee,' Mysha said, tugging at her gloves. 'That stuff at the conference is shit.'

Lieve didn't bother replying. Conference coffee was always shit.

'So he's meeting someone, right? He must be.'

Lieve shrugged. It seemed increasingly likely. The more likely it became, the more dodgy their escapade began to seem.

'We shouldn't both be facing him,' she said. 'You should face the other way'

'Why me?'

'He'll be more likely to recognise you.'

Mysha grunted, or huffed, or something, but she turned to look down the Hartenstraat. She backed herself into Lieve, as if for warmth.

Lieve's tummy rumbled.

They had grabbed a selection of sandwiches and snacks from the lunch offering at the conference before they left. Her panel was at two thirty, and she did not want to be late for it. She watched as Jaap held his phone up in front of him, then turned his head from side to side, and rearranged his scarf and his hair, letting it fall forward, then flicking it back.

She laughed.

'What?'

'Nothing.'

She was worried what would happen if Mysha did try to seduce him. She had no way of knowing how serious she was being, nor did she know how Jaap would react. He was on the flirtatious side, certainly, but that was just his manner. His occasional comments about what he did at weekends and on holidays were clearly intended to be mysterious, and the easiest course was to assume his love life was just as exciting as he wanted them to think it was. She would have felt sorry for him if it wasn't. Sleeping with students was another matter. It hadn't occurred to her that it was something that still went on, but then she wasn't the kind of person who would know if it was.

Her phone went, in her bag, and she took it out. It was Mysha. A text.

So what would you do if I did shag him?

Lieve shook her head, as if to herself, though she could feel, through her coat, in her shoulders, that Mysha felt the movement too. Lieve took off a glove and thumbed out a reply.

It's nothing to do with me what you do.

She watched as the phone lassoed her words in a little speech bubble and slipped them up the screen. It made its sending-text sound, like a tiny car whooshing past, and almost immediately came the sound of the message appearing on Mysha's phone, a little synthetic three-note bauble. Lieve looked up across the canal. Then came the whoosh of Mysha's phone and the ting of hers.

Even as she was reading the message: I've got a terrible feeling it's going to happen, with the purple devil emoji again, there came the whoosh again and the ting and under it appeared, pushing the last words up the screen: Don't look round.

She looked round.

Jenny exchanged glances with a woman stood next to the next canal – if you could exchange glances with someone wearing sunglasses, a pulled-down beanie hat and a scarf wrapped up over her mouth. She walked past her, looking carefully this time left and right before crossing the road to the bridge. The proximity of the pulsing blue circle to the red pin on her phone told her she was nearly there, and indeed there he was, Jaap, sitting at a table outside the café.

He stood as she arrived. She took off her gloves and they shook hands. They had already shaken hands that morning.

'Hello. Thanks for coming.'

She made a gesture, dismissive and self-dismissive at once, letting the fingers of her gloves – which were leather, very thin and fine – flop over her hand.

'What would you like to drink?'

'A coffee, please.'

'I guess you're feeling the jet lag. Black coffee? White? Latte? Sugar?'

'Black, thank you. No sugar.'

He went down the steps to the café and she took a seat across from his cup and cigarette packet. Twenty pounds to seduce this man. Well, it could be done, that was reasonably clear. And who was to say that it might not be interesting, if only to see how Frankie responded to it. The thought displeased her, though. However genuine the cat's intention, the owner never much likes having a dead bird laid at their feet. It was doable, but was it worth doing? It seemed to her, now, that she only the energy left for one distinctive and decisive act, to realign her life to its true course and give the faith and energy to pursue it.

She twisted on the bench to look across the brick-paved street to the chained-off canal. The sun was on her face. The city arrayed itself tastefully, as always. She looked along the buildings on the opposite bank. What she liked, most of all, was the way that the gingerbread-house gables found an echo in the design of the stoops below – she thought that was the word – the short stone platforms in any case built in front of the houses' front doors, that were reached by short staircases rising from the pavement on the left and the right. It was quaint, like an English cottage row was quaint, but at the same time it was thoroughly urban. Amsterdam was like a Paris for the pocket, a Paris reconfigured to the scale of a Cotswolds market town. And yet it was also like New York, obviously, but a New York that ordinary people could afford to live in, and cycle around, on their ordinary bicycles. She followed a pair of cyclists as they rode the length of the street across the way.

It was the canals, above all, that did it. Their primary contribution to the lived environment was the distance they gave from which to watch the houses, and that they gave the houses to watch you back, from the huge windows that dominated their facades. The simplicity of the design, married to that particular trait of the Dutch character that meant people left their windows uncurtained, made the houses a fascinating theatrical backdrop to the streets, a silent film running behind a play.

The house directly opposite, like many of the others, gave over its first storey to a single room, and the front wall of it to two huge, near ceiling-height windows. This one, unlike its neighbours, had someone at home in it. It was a woman, perhaps in her sixties, dressed in slim dark trousers and a cream top of some kind. As Jenny watched, she walked in and out of the room, through doorways at the side and at the rear, unhurriedly but somewhat aimlessly, as if she were looking for something.

Jaap re-emerged with a wide white cup in one hand and, in the other, a little round plastic tray bearing two small glasses. The glasses were filled to the brim, and the clear liquid glistened menacingly. Jaap passed Jenny the coffee, then carefully placed one of the glasses on the table in front of her. It sat in the middle of one of the thick slats; the gaps between them would be enough to tilt and spill it.

'This is for me to apologise for earlier. Jenever, like your name.' He looked at her, but she gave him no response. He seemed to shrug this off, however, with what might have been excess self-confidence, might just have been insouciance. 'Dutch gin, you know? The coffee here is good, but this will put steel in your...' he sucked his fingers and set the other glass next to his own cup, then sat down. 'In your intellect. You have had it before?'

Jenny shook her head.

'It's very cold, the glasses come straight from the freezer. You should drink like this.' He bent forwards, hands flat on the table, bringing his mouth slowly to the glass, lips puckered, until he was able to take a sip. He looked quite ridiculous, like an adult apple-bobbing, or a horse at a trough. Then, just for a moment, his eyes lifted to hers, and he looked like someone doing something else, something quite obscene – especially, she thought, considering the fact he had just named the drink for her. She picked up her coffee cup and looked away as she tried to take a drink, but had to settle for blowing on it, for it was still too hot.

'Thank you for coming,' he said, when he had sat himself back down on his bench. 'I know you're busy, and it was an unusual request. I was hoping to see you at the delegates' dinner last night.'

He had said this to her already.

She said nothing.

'But, of course, you are busy. I know how things are.'

Again, she said nothing, and he tugged a touch self-consciously at his scarf.

Perhaps feeling a little sorry for him, she reached out to touch the jenever glass with her fingertips. It was indeed cold. Tradition or no tradition, she was not going to bend herself over to drink it. She took the glass by the rim and raised it slowly to her mouth. The coldness, against the heat of the coffee, burned her lips, but there was an agreeable herby taste that came in under it. She kept the glass at her lips, then tipped it up to drink the whole of the rest of it in one go. The kick of it was strong and clear, like having something broken against the inside of her throat. She replaced the glass on the table with a tiny two-part thump and, in an involuntary gesture, placed her fingers on her neck, behind her ear.

'Very good. You like it?'

'Perfect.' She swallowed and widened her eyes, then laughed, pleased that she had been able to drink it down without coughing or wincing. 'Wow. Jeepers. Who was it that said that alcohol has the unedifying effect of making one feel more human?'

'I don't know, but I approve of the sentiment.'

For a beat neither of them spoke, but looked out, in parallel, at the road and the canal. People passed by, on foot and on cycle. An expensive car, low to the ground, tottered forward. In the other direction, a seagull, taking a bead down the centre of the waterway, as if on its daily commute. Jenny looked again for the woman in the house across the canal. She seemed to have found what she was looking for, for she had taken a seat looking out through one of the windows, and was reading, holding a book up in front of her face; perhaps it was her book she had been looking for, or her glasses.

Jaap, she saw, had followed her gaze and was watching the woman too.

'What must it be like,' she said, 'to live your life like this, on permanent show. It's such a Dutch thing.'

'It is certainly a 'Dam thing,' he said. 'She is quite magnificent, isn't she?'

'What I can't work out is what it says about the Dutch character, to be like this. If it suggests intense humility, and a modesty as to one's place in the world – that one doesn't care or mind about being seen, and she doesn't consider herself on show at all – or if it suggests intense narcissism, exhibitionism, even. That one insists on it, on being seen.'

'Perhaps it is precisely in our pride at our own sense of humility that the Dutch narcissism lies. A hangover from the Golden Age, the Gouden Eeuw – though I'm afraid your friend Frankie had it a little wrong. The gold of our Golden Age was not the warm misty moral glow of the Classicists. It was hard currency.' He rubbed the fingers and thumb of one hand together. 'It was capitalism in action. And the open windows were to show you weren't spending it on fripperies. Pride in your godliness. A very Protestant sin. If that's not too glib a way to say it. Do I mean glib? Is that the right word?'

'Yes. Yes it is, and yes it was. But still, it's not half as glib as what I'm going to say next.'

She was aware that the gin had loosened her tongue a little. This early in the day, and on top of the jet lag. She felt ready for it, however, whatever it was. He offered her his cigarette packet.

'No, thank you. Glib.' She tried out the word again. 'Glib, glibber, glibbest. Glibber. My god, that must be the worst word in the English language.'

It must have been strong, the jenever. She toyed with the glass, but kept her eyes on the woman opposite.

'Totally not fit for purpose,' she went on. 'I doubt it's been used in anger in decades.'

'So if that is the worst word, then what is the best? What, personally, is your favourite word?'

She looked at him, at the way he was holding himself, the pleasure he was taking in smoking his cigarette, or perhaps the pleasure he was exhibiting through it. The way he handled it, the way he turned his head to exhale, was subtly triumphant, almost as if it was post-coital. She felt glad to be in a country where people smoked again. She felt angry at Frankie for encouraging her to even come to meet him, when she had so much else to be doing – working on her speech, salvaging it, raking something out of the ashes – and yet that anger had turned into a kind of pleasure at being here, like they were playing truant. She took her gloves from the table and pulled them back on, flexing her fingers to push them into their sockets. She was very tired.

'The best word,' she said. 'I've always had a soft spot for pulmonary embolism. It rather trips off the tongue, doesn't it?'

Then she realised what she'd said, and groaned inwardly. He nodded, as if taking her seriously, the idiot, and repeated the words. 'Pulmonary embolism. Was that your thought, then? You were going to tell me your' – he paused – 'glibber thought.'

'Yes, no, I was.' She drank some coffee. She felt like the situation was getting out of hand, and that it was only by keeping talking that she could keep herself under control. 'Well, we were talking about how you Dutch live your lives all on show. Christ, you even display your shit to yourselves, the way your toilets are designed. Whereas we Brits are compulsive net curtain-twitchers. Well, what that reminds me of, what she reminds me of' – gesturing to the woman across the canal – 'is your red light district. Only what's for sale is not sex, but instead enlightened bourgeois liberalism.

'I speak from memory of course, possibly even from folk memory. The red light district, I mean. It might not even be like that anymore. The idea that you knock on a window, ask the prices, discuss terms, all out in the open. I feel it's the same with our friend over there. I could go over, knock on her window. Ask her what she does, how much she earns, who her favourite clothes designers and politicians and authors and artists are, and if I like it, we talk terms, and then I can basically walk in and have her life.'

She looked at him, offering him his turn to speak.

'Well, I think you might be overstating the influence of liberal humanism in the Netherlands just at the moment. There is plenty about our country that you wouldn't want to buy into blind, as it were. But the whores, they're still there.' He smiled to say the word, framing the sound of it with his mouth. 'They're not called that any more, as I'm sure you know, but then, well, I suppose whore is one of my favourite words.' He ashed his cigarette. 'It has its roots, naturally you know this, in the Proto-Indo-European qar, from which source you get words like carus, Latin, dear; cara, old Irish, friend.'

'Cariad, in the Welsh.'

'Cariad, yes. Also Kamah, in the Sanskrit: love, desire. Follow it through to Proto-Germanic, and you get khoraz, khoron, one who desires. Why are you smiling?'

She was smiling, though obviously she couldn't say this, at his guttural fricatives, the thick grating in the throat at the kh sound – the same noise that had sounded so grisly over pancakes just an hour ago. She reached across with her gloved hand and pulled out with a leather fingertip a cigarette from his packet lying open on the table, one of those old-fashioned soft-top packs, without the hinged lid. She enjoyed how the material of the glove adhered to the paper wrapping of the cigarette, offering just enough friction to slide it softly out. She picked up the cigarette and put it in her mouth. He leaned across towards her with his lighter, but only halfway, so she had to lean back to meet him. She did so, almost demurely, resting her gloved fingers on his wrist as he lit her. She leaned back and inhaled.

'Anyway,' he went on. 'I approve of the legal approach to whoring, though clearly more needs to be done with regards to trafficking, etcetera, but the cultural shift is very slow. I think people, by which I mean us, the Dutch, hoped that with legalisation it would somehow disappear. If other countries had followed suit perhaps it would have. Or not disappeared, but become invisible, part of the ordinary fabric of society. Not this... silly joke for tourists. The same goes for the drugs. The law itself is fine, but because you other countries are twenty years behind, your idiot students come over here and clutter up the gutters of our beautiful city.

In their fucking stupid hats.'

He went on: 'But your point about our windows is true. We are a northern people, and we like the light, we need it.'

'What about you? Do you live like that?'

'Sure I do. And you? Could you live like that?' Could you?'

It felt like a challenge.

She turned her head to exhale.

Which felt like a defeat.

'There was something you wanted to show me,' she said.

'Yes. But first, about this morning. I wanted to say again I'm sorry. I handled it badly.'

'It was I who handled it badly. I didn't know that Leonard has cancer, and I am finding it difficult to deal with that fact. I'm very tired, and I've got jet lag and I can't help finding my behaviour repulsive, and desperately sad.'

'I don't think it's repulsive. It's understandable.'

'Jaap – am I saying that right? Jaap? I didn't say it wasn't understandable. I said it was repulsive. But, Jaap, if you want to help me, to make amends for accidentally triggering my self-sadness, what would help is not consolation, but distraction.'

'Very well.' He stood up. 'This I can do. And in fact, what I have to show you is very much linked to this woman.' He nodded across the canal. 'I am going to show you a woman, in a room, very much like that one.'

'A woman in a room.'

'And a man, in fact. But mostly the woman.'

'Seriously?'

'Seriously. It's nothing bad, honest. I think you'll like it.'

'OK, then.'

They gathered their things, and went over the bridge and

along the street on the far side of the canal. They passed directly underneath the apartment, which had a small bench in front of the raised stoop, chained to a railing. She looked up, but at this angle the woman was invisible, the windows obliquely opaque.

They walked two more blocks along the canal. They didn't talk. She let him walk ahead of her, and watched him as they went. Eventually he stopped and took a set of keys from his jacket pocket. The house they were outside was of a similar design, merely a different shade of dark brown brick framing the great tall windows. This time the door was down some steps from the street, with stained glass behind a protective grille. He rang the buzzer, waited a long moment, then unlocked the door.

'Hallo,' he called, then turned to talk to Jenny. 'This isn't my house. It's the home of a friend, whose dog I walk when she is away, so I have a key. Just now she is – I think – at work.'

She followed him into the hallway, one hand tight on her handbag strap, and wondering to herself as she went. The very weirdness of the moment made it seem plausible.

A small brown and white spaniel skittered into view at the top of the staircase and looked down at them. It barked, twice, then retreated a pace and sat. Jaap called again, then set off up the stairs, and she went after him. Always following people up sets of stairs, she thought to herself, and never knowing what's at the top. At the top Jaap bent to tousle the spaniel and speak to it – the dog seemed happy enough to see him – then they went along the landing that doubled back towards the front of the house: Jaap, Jenny, the dog.

At the door to the front room he stood aside to let her walk in ahead of him. She did so delicately, perhaps anticipating how he wanted her to experience it, like she was walking into an art exhibit. The light from the front windows cut slantwise across the boarded wooden floor to paint a vertical section of the wall next to the door. What furniture there was, was in dark wood. A mahogany sideboard held a pair of large lacquered bowls, one half-filled with potpourri, the other with coins and keys with coloured tags and plastic covers.

She turned towards the windows at the front, and looked out through them, partly, she thought, to provoke Jaap, if they were indeed here as trespassers, and partly to hold back her thoughts about the room, to dam them, let them keep their power. She looked both ways along the canal. As usual there were people passing, on bicycles, on foot, singly and in pairs. Nobody noticed her, up in the window. Another tourist boat, largely empty. The houses opposite, nobody in their windows.

Jaap was standing behind her, waiting, but she was in no hurry. She stayed facing out of the window and reconstructed the room in her mind. There were two upright chairs, she knew, towards the front of the room, but facing back into it. Against the left wall was the sideboard, the bowls on the sideboard. Hanging beside it, a mirror. At the back of the room, on the other side, a doorway opening onto a back room. Next to the doorway, in the middle of the back wall, there was a painting.

6

The painting itself was not large, but in its heavy frame it seemed so. The wood of the frame was the colour of old church pews, with thin grooves to it that caught and held the light in long vertical lines. It was not the only painting in the room – there was a miniature on the wall by the door to the landing, a floral composition of some kind – but this was the one that drew the eye.

It was a Golden Age interior, the like of which you might see a dozen times in the Rijksmuseum, Jenny guessed, and once or twice in any gallery in Europe or America with a half-decent collection to its name. Its subject was simple, domestic: a woman and a man in a room, that might have been a parlour or reception room, a public-facing room in any event, rather than a bedroom or a kitchen. It seemed well-appointed, though far from showy. The most striking thing about it was the yellow and black tiled floor that spread in expanding diamonds towards the viewer. There were paintings on the walls of the room in the painting, and a mirror on the left wall, tilted so that it reflected the tiles in a flourish of perspective that doubtless the painter had been particularly pleased with.

The woman in the painting had her back towards the viewer, and in her right hand she held a letter. She was looking towards the door in the back wall of the room, through which you could see the end of a simple wooden bed and the corner of a curtained and leaded window that let daylight in; a barred parallelogram of it stretched across the floor and into the main room, cutting across the diamond pattern of the tiles and making them shine.

The woman's face was shown in the merest profile, just the point of the nose and the crest of the cheek, such that you felt yourself impelled to move, or even just lean a little, so as to see her more clearly. She was holding herself as if about to take a step, as if she'd just heard someone in the next room; her centre of gravity was such that you felt she couldn't *not* move, had committed herself to movement. Her left hand was resting on the shoulder of her companion, who was sitting on a chair.

He, the man, sat looking straight out of the painting, meeting the viewer's gaze with an expression of jovial inscrutability that couldn't help also seeming insufferably smug, as if he knew he was in a painting and she didn't, and this gave him some kind of advantage over her.

Both of them were dressed in what seemed to Jenny the standard bourgeois garb of the age: for the woman, a grey full-length dress, cinched at the waist, and a white, shapeless bonnet covering the hair and ear, the dress with plain white collars, rather than lacework. You could see the toe of one shoe peeking out from underneath the hem at the bottom.

He wore a black jacket with more flamboyant collar and cuffs, and black breeches with white stockings. The square metal buckles on his shoes flashed at the viewer. He had his wide-brimmed hat on his knee, and his black-grey locks – a wig? she never knew if these things were wigs or real hair – tumbled over his shoulders like some terrible rock star perm from the 1970s. The collar and cuffs and hat were the painting's only visible marks of ostentation. There was a sideboard or dresser to one side, and something that might have been a bird cage hung up high on the wall, under the dark ceiling, but the wall was plainly painted plaster, with no hangings. The chair he was sitting on was austere – a simple kitchen chair – but he sat confidently, one arm hooked over the back, one leg languidly extended to show off the curve of the calf, the hat tipping decorously off the knee of the other.

Jenny moved her gaze away from the painting. There, to its right, was the doorway to a further room, at the back of the house. Through the doorway you could see the corner of a bed. She caught and held her breath, not quite trusting her eyes, or her ability to process properly the information they gave her. There was a window through there too, with a curtain more or less the same colour and weight of that in the picture.

She took a step back and looked again, and gasped out a laugh that, instinctively, she swallowed back. Yes, it was true.

The painting was placed in the room such that the viewer stood not right in front of it, but a few yards back, in what she supposed was the natural viewing position, found herself in relation to it as the woman in the painting did to the room she was in.

And
the
door
lead
ing to
the
bac
k ro
om
was
som
ewhe
e ove
here

The   pai
ntin   g
you   mig
ht   say
was   hun
g   about
h   e   r   e

wh
ile
she
was s
ome w
here o
ver he
re, sta
ndi ng
lo ok
in g.

The mirror was there, in the room in the painting, as it was in the room she stood in: both of them tilted down at the same angle, one reflecting tiles, the other floorboards. There was the end of the sideboard, too, she now saw, in the left-hand corner of the painting, with its dark wood bowl, though presumably without bright plastic key fobs in it. She had a momentary jolt of panic that there might be, and the painting revealed as a foul meticulous fake, but of course there wasn't.

And yes, the dress. Hers, though shorter at the knee and more fitted in the bust, was of the same colour and even perhaps roughly the same material as the dress of the woman in the painting, even down to the collar. Her dress, bought last month in a Rockridge boutique, might have been inspired by the picture. She was glad, at least, of her boots; they proved her individuality.

She looked round. Jaap was standing to the side and just behind her, looking with her at the painting – but his attention, she could tell, was on the painting only insofar as it was the focus of hers. Otherwise, his attention was all on her. Behind him, the spaniel, sitting patiently, tongue out, ears hanging.

'It's a wonderful painting,' she said.

'It is.'

'It's done so nicely. It could so easily have been a gimmick. If they had replicated the tiles on the floor, for instance, your friend.'

'It could.'

'Or if there had been a dog in the painting.'

'A dog.'

'I'm joking.'

'Thank you. Yes, a dog.'

'The temptation to do that. The importance of not doing it. It makes me think of Dali, with his room made up to be Mae West's face. So silly. Painters who insist on manhandling their viewers into a particular position with regards to their paintings. I don't approve.' She looked back at the picture. 'Paintings aren't movies, they're rooms. You're allowed to walk around them. Please don't tell me anything about it, by the way. I'm enjoying not having the little card telling me everything I need to know about it. My eye keeps drifting down there. It's an instinctive reaction.'

She raised her right hand and traced a movement in the air, a reading of the painting; starting with the letter in the woman's hand, and moving in a tight spiral round to the right and down across the lower portion of her dress to her hand on the man's shoulder, and then up past the indistinct picture on the wall – that took the place of the picture itself in the room, this room, their room – and up to the top corner of the doorway into the back room.

She sketched a second, different arc in the other direction. There were lines real and implied cutting every which way across the painting, as if it were caught within the frames of more than one order of perspective, like one of those strange Escher worlds.

'You like it?' he said, speaking carefully, quietly.

'I love it.'

'I love the way you can't see her face. What is she thinking? You want to see her face.'

'Is she beautiful.'

'Yes. If you could see her face, you think, the mystery of the painting, what's in the letter, would be solved.'

'The question of contingency applies, you might say.'

'You might say that. There is much to say about it.'

His voice, to be sure, was compelling, seductive even. His English had the usual American taint – a sort of rise or lift to the middle of the words – and then there was the Dutch slur, making him sound as though he had a mild speech impediment, or was slightly drunk.

'What I find so strange is that it's unclear if we are dealing with allegory or realism. Is the scene general and emblematic, or specific and individual, with its own narrative peculiarity? Do we care about these two people? Do we judge them? Do we want to know what happens to them? Are they, in fact, characters, or merely figures?'

Jenny adjusted her pose so it more closely echoed that of the woman in the painting. Her left hand raised, the one that would be resting on the shoulder of the seated figure, the right out by her side, open, as if holding a letter. With her gaze directed towards the next room, the painting was now only visible in her peripheral vision; it burred there, like a premonition, as nearly in view as the woman's face was in the painting itself.

She allowed herself to settle into the moment. A room inside the room.

She tried to perceive herself, in the room – the room she was in – and imagine how she looked, standing there. She felt like she was a key, a final piece to a puzzle that was waiting to be slotted in.

If you took the logic of it seriously, the logic of whoever had put this painting here, and arranged the room around it, you would have to assume there was another person, someone else, behind her, not with them in the room, but entirely outside of its frame, outside its order of perspective, as this room was outside the frame of the room contained in the painting. And that person, in whatever extravagant exploded dimension it would take to turn the room she was in into a picture, or an object of aesthetic perception, would be looking at the room she herself was standing in, and looking at the back of her head, at the tip of her nose and the crest of her cheek – she adjusted her head so that was all that could be seen by them – and they would be wondering about her and her actions and intentions, trying to guess them from her not-quite-visible face, just as she was considering those of the bonneted woman.

It took all of her will to not turn around and look for them, look them squarely in the face. She wanted to do it.

She wanted to turn around and look at that person and address them, as she imagined the woman in the painting, if she were given the ability to do so, would want to turn and address her, anyone looking at her. She wanted to tell them, you don't know what's going on in my head. My thoughts and desires and intentions are not yours to know. They are barely mine to know myself, and I'm not going to let you near them.

The pad and squeak of his shoes on the wood, the sound of a chair being lifted.

'You don't mind?' Jaap said.

She moved her head, held her hand steady. She bristled with the thought of being looked at, wondered about, perceived, implicated; of being a person in a room, or in a picture of a room.

The chair was placed, and he sat upon it. She listened to the sound of a body arranging itself in space, its posture, its limbs. There, now, she felt it: the smooth and bobbled fabric of his jacket under her hand. He was now looking directly out of the painting, if this room they were in were a painting, at the hypothetical viewer, whoever that was. She relaxed herself a touch, allowed herself to relax, like a boat coming into dock. She did not want to feel as if she were play-acting. The moment, the correspondence, was close enough as it was.

She thought of that rather formal Elizabethan dancing you saw in historical films, in which people turned genteel pirouettes, touching each other by the lightest handhold, and spoke important dialogue to each other as they danced, without ever quite looking directly at one another.

'What is in her letter, do you suppose?' she said, aware of formality of her speech, of its utter distance from any kind of flirtatiousness. 'And if you do suppose, then is your supposition based on fact or convention?'

'There's no convention that I know of. I could tell you the title of the painting but that would add nothing. It was most likely added long after the painting was finished in any case. Personally, I always took it to show a husband who has found out his wife's adultery.'

'Oh.'

'That's what letters usually stand for in this kind of painting. He has discovered the letter, and shown it to his wife, and he's smiling at the viewer, because he knows he is once more back on top, as it were.'

'Not the usual response of a cuckold, you'd think.'

'You have to remember this is the Netherlands, in the seventeenth century. It is not eighteenth-century France. Discovering her infidelity – which might not even be infidelity as we understand it; might be nothing more than a love letter, to her, full of airy declarations – this puts him in a stronger, not a weaker position.'

'True. He is looking very pleased with himself. And yet she is the one with the letter. She is the active agent, here. The one moving, about to move. She is about to act, not him. It could equally be his letter, to or from a lover, that she has discovered. Which would explain his expression just as well.'

'And if she is going to the next room, then perhaps she is taking him to bed.'

She shook her head, as much to dislodge the thought as to disagree with it.

'The bed is a red herring,' she said. 'I don't think this is a seduction we're talking about.'

Then, in quick succession, so quick in fact that it was unclear in which order they came, she – they – heard the sound of the dog scampering out to the landing; and the dog barking; and, from below, the front door opening.

She looked at him, alarmed, in time to see he was just as surprised as she was, though the sight of her spooked moved him quickly to an expression of pleasure, which consequently made her scowl. The dog barked again, clattering down the stairs, and she heard a voice, a woman's voice, speaking in Dutch. 'Hallo,' it called, then something else, a phrase, a question, uncertain – is there anyone there? presumably, or something like it – then more words, but quieter, directed to the dog, as if she was bending to talk to it.

Jaap took Jenny by the arm and led her to the rear door and then into the back room. It was half bedroom, half, it seemed, study. There was a single bed, made up and unslept in, a desk and a chair. An old desktop computer. Books and box files. There was the window, with its view onto a smaller back street: residential, cobbled, lined with bollards and potted trees and plants set either side of the ground-floor doorways.

Jaap pressed himself against the wall, next to the doorway, and pulled Jenny alongside him. They had their backs to the wall and it occurred to her that she was directly behind the painting, with nothing between it and her but a few centimetres of plaster, wood and void. Jaap had his finger to his lips, a sign to keep silent, but he was smiling, also. They were close enough that she could feel his breath on her chin and cheek. He smelt of cigarette, but then so did she, most likely. He moved his head sideways along the wall towards her and whispered, his lips brushing her hair he spoke: 'I think we're OK. She probably thinks she didn't double-lock the door this morning.'

'What if she's come home for the afternoon?'

'No. She's just here to collect something for her work.' Then, when Jenny looked questioningly at him. 'She told the dog. She said it to the dog when she came in.' She took this in. 'She'll go again soon.'

'Couldn't you just go and say you're here? This is silly.'

'Silly? I don't think it's silly.'

But then there was the sound of footsteps on the stairs, steady human ones and frantic canine ones. She pressed herself against the wall, felt the solidity of it in her shoulder blades, the scratch of her hair clip against it, the bump of the back of her head; she looked out at the house opposite, wondered if there was anyone home there, what they would think if they looked out to see them here, hiding like children, or burglars.

She could hear the woman talking to her dog, a sort of

low, hearty shushing.

He didn't want to go out and confront his friend, she thought, because she was here. He didn't want his friend to see her – or her to see his friend. There had been a photograph hung in the hallway, a black and white shot of a woman, somewhere outside, against a hillside or mountainside, long thick hair that held itself in unruly waves, an open, laughing mouth, but she had seen it only in passing, as they climbed the stairs, and of course there was no guarantee it was her.

Then the footsteps were in the room, the squeak of the shoe and the soft reply of the wood. They stopped. She felt Jaap tense, his body braced as if for movement. He was about to step around and out through the door to reveal himself, she thought, and she bridled at the thought of him giving himself up like that, the words he would say to excuse them, words that she wouldn't be able to understand: that's what annoyed her most. She wouldn't have him putting her in that position.

She moved a hand to cover his, to hold him still.

It seemed to work. His body didn't relax, exactly, but it relented. They remained where they were, the two of them. They, too – the other two, next door, on the other side of the wall – remained where they were. The only sound was the sound of the panting dog and, for Jenny, the bass drum thud of her heart in her chest and the roar of blood and thought in the ducts of her head.

She was standing, this woman, where she had stood three minutes before. She was looking at the painting. She spoke, a mumbled half-sentence with a rising, ironical inflection, to the dog or to herself, though the dog didn't answer. Jenny concentrated on her hand, on Jaap's hand in or under hers. She was alert to any movement from him that might communicate or translate what the woman was saying, but he was silent, and still.

Then there were sounds of movement from the room, and for a terrible, knife-sharp second it was unclear if the woman, walking, was walking towards them or away from them; for that terrible second it could have been either, was both, and panic broke out in her chest in response.

But it was away, it was away. Yes, it was. The woman's foot squeaked on the turn, at the door, and she was back out on the landing – separated from them for a moment by a different wall – and then she was gone.

Jenny exhaled; she felt herself descend in height by half a centimetre; her eyelids blinked and fluttered.

The sound of the stairs being descended.

The two of them turned, giving each other sight of their shared and individual senses of relief, anger, release, excitement. In turning he had taken her hand in his. They were both smiling. She lifted her other hand and placed it on his cheek and jaw, thumb on his lip, fingers extended towards his ear. She drew the ball of her thumb across the scratch of his stubble. He began to move, very softly, turning his mouth towards her hand; in response she pressed harder, to stop him, so she held him by the jaw. She had her eyes opened very wide, not so much to look at him as to make it clear that she was doing so.

'I am serious,' he said, in a whisper. 'I am a serious man. Please don't think I am frivolous, or silly.'

It was her word, she heard it in his manner of speaking it; he was quoting her.

She moved his head, turning it with her hand, not roughly, but not gently either, this way and that. He let her turn it. She turned it away from her, so that she could see him in profile, consider him like that. She imagined having Frankie's face in her hand like this, imagined her face in Frankie's hands. They were appealing thoughts. Perhaps this man could be preparation for Frankie, a warm-up session, like young girls were supposed to kiss each other as practice for boys.

'I'm in the country for two days,' she said. 'I have old friends to catch up with. Some of them, as you know, will take a lot of catching up with. Perhaps they can't be caught. I like that you brought me here, Jaap. I like your painting that isn't yours. I loved seeing it, and I find you interesting, though perhaps not as interesting as you would like. I don't think this is a seduction, however.' She pushed his head a little further, so it was pressed sideways against the wall, facing away from her. 'We are not the people in the painting. No one is watching us. There is no narrative to be inferred.'

He smiled, and she felt the muscles in his jaw move, and felt for a moment that she knew how it would be to be blind, and to read people this way, through touch and sound alone.

Now he did turn his face towards her – she let him turn it – so they were looking at each other, both of them resting the sides of their heads against the wall. Both of them, she knew, were still listening hard, both interpreting the sounds from downstairs as the woman moved about, talking quietly to the dog.

'Perhaps so,' he said. 'Though seduction can take many forms. I was seduced by the introduction to a single academic paper.'

'Is that so?' she said.

Very slowly, very carefully, and watching her for her reaction, he moved his free arm so it came past her cheek, and then she felt the release, like a knot untied, as he unclamped the clip that held tight her hair, so that it fell in uneven stages down her head and onto her back. Then his fingers were in her hair. They insinuated themselves, worked their way in, then rested there, giving her time to tell him to stop. Then, when she didn't, he pushed his hand through the length of it, drawing it out and down, losing his fingers in it, measuring it, almost tugging it when they came to the end.

She knew what he was doing, even if he didn't. It was not Frankie, but her husband who had awoken to her the idea of hair as a site of desire. There was nothing quite like human hair, he had told her, well-washed and conditioned and sleek with natural and processed oils, to evoke the female sex in a state of arousal. The give and take of tissue, grain and slickness. The hiddenness and unnavigability of it. When I have my hands in your hair, he'd said to her, on more than one occasion, it's like I have my hand in your cunt. It had been, on occasion, an arousing thought. It was now.

She allowed her head to shift forwards, sliding along the wall so that she felt the texture of it against her ear, still listening, until their mouths were contiguous, one next to the other, the skin of their cheeks in communication. The fingers in her hair were still, as if his hand had died. She relaxed the muscles in her calves so her upper lip came to rest in the opening of his mouth, her lips around his lower lip, his lips around her upper.

She had little interest in kissing, as a sexual practice. It did nothing for her, erotically, but then she hadn't kissed anyone in over two years, and this was not unpleasant, no matter that their mouths, jointly, tasted foul. So she kissed him. She kissed him for what might have been half a minute, and then went on kissing him for might have been two. A measured dialogue of advances, retreats, and parlays, all at the level of microevent, a traffic and exchange of sour breath. They continued until, at last, there came the decisive clunk of the front door, the tug on the handle to check.

She drew back – just an inch, but it was enough. Her lips rang with raw sensation. He drew back, too, obediently, but tightened his fingers in her hair. She shook her head, to acknowledge him, and to shrug him off, and he removed his hand. They were still standing close, still leaning against the wall, she on her right side, he on his left.

'There,' he said. 'I am seduced, completely.'

'You are more than seduced. This has been a relationship, entire. If a seduction can last the length of a conversation, then a relationship can last the length of a kiss. Once upon a time we met, once upon a time we kissed, once upon a time we found it time to part.' She waggled her fingers in front of his face, in between their faces, not without coquettishness. 'I absolve you of your desire.'

He dipped his forehead to brush against her fingers. The expression on his face was that of someone allowing himself to be tamed. He was intelligent enough, and had enough imagination, she thought, to accept it. This was no true absolution though, she knew. She had subdued it, as if by enchantment. It was safely asleep, but it could be woken again. She felt sure that it was in her gift alone to wake it. His expression told her all this.

'The thing is,' she said, 'that at present, I'm just not very interested in people.'

'Well, there's your problem. That is in itself an interesting thing to say. Perhaps I'm interested in people who aren't interested in people.'

She looked at him, trying to work out if there was more to what he said than it seemed. 'Well, good luck with that,' she said, then righted herself from the wall, smoothed her dress and walked past him and through the door into the outer room.

There she stopped.

He, coming out, stopped beside her.

Together they saw it.

The chair: there, where they'd left it, clearly moved from its home by the window, turned to face its fellow, as if under interrogation. Draped over it, his scarf.

'Fuck. Shit,' he said. 'It's not funny.'

Jenny ran a finger under her nose.

'Oh, believe me. It's very funny.'

Good laughter was like a draught of clean water, honest and invigorating.

'You'll notice I'm not asking who she is,' she said. 'Your friend with the beautiful painting.'

He went to the window and peered out, looking down at the street.

'Verdammt. Idiot.'

She went to stand beside him. The world outside was as before. The same buildings. The same people biking and walking – tourists? Amsterdammers? The bench on the pavement opposite now had a couple of women sat on it, well wrapped up in hats and scarves, eating sandwiches.

'Don't worry,' she said.

'I'm not worried.'

'You are. You are worried what your friend will think of you. How you will explain yourself to her. She knew, didn't she? She knew we were there, in the next room? What did she even say, when she was there?'

He picked up the scarf and looped it angrily around his neck.

'Don't answer me, then.'

'She didn't say anything that would have meant she definitely knew we were there. I wouldn't just have stood there if she had.' He looked at his watch, pulled a sour face. 'We should be getting back. The panel I'm chairing at two thirty has this student I emailed you about, Lieve Braam.' Then, when he saw her expression, 'That's right. I remember. Things have been hectic.' His expression was just short of being sarcastic, but not, she thought, bitter.

'I'm sorry.'

'You should come. She's really good. You'll like what she's doing.'

Jenny pulled a grimacing face.

'Sorry. I've really got to work on my speech for tomorrow. It's terrible, I know, but I just need to take a look at it.'

'Well, OK. That's a shame. Perhaps I can introduce you anyway.'

'Of course.'

'You will come back to the conference when you're done? Things will be livening up from about five o'clock. It's... well, it'll be fun, I think.'

'Of course. I just need an hour or two.'

'Good. Shall we go?'

He moved the treasonous chair back to its original

position, took a last look around the room, and went out onto the landing. Jenny went after him. They left the house and he locked the front door, then they set off, following the canal again. Jenny asked him to tell her more about his student, really out of a sense of obligation, but he was distracted, frowning as he looked across the canal. There were two women, she saw, walking, some way ahead of them, on the opposite bank. She recognised them, from their hats and scarves. They were the ones that had been sat on the bench opposite.

Jaap sped up. One of the women looked around, saw them, and she spoke to her companion and they, too, began to hurry. Jenny had to quicken her pace to keep up with Jaap, who was walking now with urgency. The canal-side street ran a good hundred yards more until the next bridge.

'Those women. They were outside the house, sitting opposite.'

'Two of my students,' Jaap replied, shortly. He started to half-jog, alternating brief runs and powerful long strides. He turned to speak to her as he went. 'Sorry, look. I need to talk to them. I'll see you later, back at the university. Sorry. This is...'

He didn't complete the thought. Jenny slackened her pace and let him outpace her. He would have to hurry to get to the bridge and over it before they reached the corner and the side road. The two women – the two students – leaned into their walk, arm in arm, but seemed unwilling or unable to actually run. Jenny slowed further and stopped. There was, she felt, something private about this encounter, that she did not want to be party to. She felt irritated with Jaap, irritated with herself – that she had to go and work on her speech – irritated all of sudden again with the whole enterprise. There seemed no certain way forward from where she was. She took a step backwards, watching him break into a run, then another step, then turned and set off in the opposite direction.

7

'Well, what the hell are we going to do now?'

Mysha, to Lieve, walking beside her, looked frightened, and excited, and then, in what seemed like a sop to her friend, uncertain.

'I don't know,' Lieve replied. 'It was your idea. You're the one...'

'The one what?'

They spoke quietly, though urgently, for people were walking past them all the time.

'Look, what he gets up to in his own time is his own business. You're not going to tell me you thought he was some kind of monk.'

'I just want to know who she is. Christ, she's not coming with him, is she?'

Lieve's stomach lurched. She stole a quick look across the canal.

'No, I don't think so. It's just him.'

He was level with them now, as they neared the bridge.

As if as one, they turned onto it and waited by the nearside railing. He crossed towards them and stopped a few paces from where they stood. Lieve closed her hand around her phone in her pocket. It felt like a stand-off in a film, or a meeting between spies. Jaap was breathing heavily after his run, and trying not to show it. He tugged his scarf away from his throat.

'Lieve,' he said. 'Mysha.'

'Jaap.'

'Jaap.'

He looked, Lieve saw, first to her, and then to Mysha, then back to her. She took off her sunglasses and her beanie hat, thinking this would make her seem more serious. Mysha took off her sunglasses and her hat as well.

'What the hell do you think you're up to?'

Mysha began to answer – 'We were just out for a walk,' she was saying – but Lieve butted in, talking over her, speaking almost wearily. 'We followed you,' she said.

Jaap gave a brief upwards jerk of the head, in acknowledgement of her words. He seemed stumped for what to say next. His expression kept changing. He looked cross, and then he wiggled his eyebrows up and down, and then there was a goofy smile on his face, as if he was amused at the severity of the situation, or pretending to be. Come on and say something, Lieve thought. He must know how to act in these kinds of situations.

'We, I mean I. I wanted to ask you something,' Mysha said. 'We had something to ask you. We thought you would be just going out to buy cigarettes, but then you kept going so we followed you.

'I'm sorry,' she finished, and there was a meekness to her

voice that made Lieve tighten her lips.

'It's not the kind of behaviour I expect from my students,' Jaap said.

'I know,' Mysha said. 'It was stupid. I'm sorry.'

She was very good at being told off, Lieve thought. Being good at being told off is a skill. Someone who is good at it can probably get whatever they want in life.

Jaap sighed. He got out his cigarettes and took one from the packet. He went to return the pack to his pocket, but then Mysha made a reflex movement of the hand, as if in anticipation of being offered one. He held the pack out to her, then to Lieve, who said no. There was a pause while Jaap lit his cigarette, then Mysha's – Mysha, who rarely smoked. There was the sound of shared inhalations. The pause. The exhale.

The moment seemed to mark a truce of sorts. But if the cigarette was a peace offering, it also indicated a deepening and widening out of the encounter. They would not be able to leave, and go their separate ways, until the cigarettes were finished. The cigarettes meant further discussion, analysis and explanation. They fixed the incident in their shared timeline.

'You're both intelligent people,' Jaap said, presently. 'You are not just students. As postgraduate students you are members of the department, colleagues. A certain relaxing of the boundaries is natural. But there are limits. I was showing Doctor Thursley a painting that belongs to a friend of mine.'

'Oh,' said Lieve. Her stomach lurched again, and she put her hand halfway to her mouth. 'Oh shit.'

'Oh,' said Jaap, imitating her. 'Sorry, Lieve. Did you want

to speak to her? Shall I ring her?' He sounded like her father.

Jennifer Thursley's name had made no impression on Mysha. 'You were showing her a painting?' she said, teasingly, almost leeringly, as if the phrase was some kind of euphemism.

'Yes,' Jaap said. 'A painting. A Golden Age interior. Possibly by Gerard ter Borch.' He spoke ironically, jibing her for her philistinism. 'It's attributed to him, at least, but it has some remarkable features even without that. If you are interested, I'm sure I could arrange a viewing. It's a remarkable work. In any case, there is better use you can be making of your time than this.' His voice hardened. 'This is an important opportunity for you, for both of you. You should be out there, talking to people, networking. There are *plenty* of far more interesting people here today than me.'

He took a last draw on his cigarette, rubbed it along the metal railing of the bridge to extinguish it, and dropped it to the floor.

'Wait, what?' said Mysha, to Lieve. '*Who* is she?'

'Jennifer Thursley,' said Lieve. 'She's the person who wrote that stuff on international business greetings that I'm using in my paper. From Berkeley. Remember? She's brilliant. Super-smart.' She shook her head.

'Exactly, yes,' said Jaap. 'Absolutely one of the most interesting people at the entire conference.' He leaned towards Lieve. 'I *had* asked her to come along to your workshop...'

Lieve looked at the ground. She felt mortified. She tried to think of a way of asking Jaap if Jennifer Thursley knew who she was, and what she had been doing. Having her at her session would be the worst thing. She couldn't believe she had put herself in this situation.

'Right. So. Please stop fucking about. Enjoy the weekend. Are you coming back now? You've got a little time.'

'No,' said Lieve. 'You go back. We'll follow you in a bit. And sorry.'

'Well, yes,' he replied. 'But just, you know, act like adults. Take the serious stuff seriously, and then have fun when it's time to have fun.' And he did a little jig, there on the street, making his hands into fists and moving them up and down, lifting his knees in turn, a rudimentary jig. He looked like an idiot.

They waited till he was out of sight before either of them spoke.

Mysha blew out a long breath, and grinned at Lieve. 'Sh-i-it,' she said, speculatively. Lieve's response clearly wasn't what she had hoped for, however, and she rolled her eyes and pulled a face, then dropped her cigarette end onto the ground. She nudged it with her toe, so it went over the kerb into the canal.

Lieve observed the manoeuvre.

'You still want to shag him?' she said.

'More than ever. It's more of a challenge, now, isn't it?'

She pumped her fists and worked her knees, aping Jaap's dance moves.

'How so. Because of the woman?' She still didn't want to name her.

'Not woman. *Women.*'

Lieve snorted. 'You don't think they got up to anything in there, do you?'

'What, and you don't?' Mysha mimicked Jaap's voice. 'Gebrand ter Borch-di-borch. Official attribution. *Remarkable* features. Yeah, like they were looking at a bloody painting. You could practically smell it on him.'

Lieve wondered about this. She hadn't been able to smell anything. She thought about the two women, about the woman who had gone into the house, then come out again, barely ten minutes later.

'That cigarette, Lieve, darling, was post-coital, believe me. Bet you she's a regular conference shag.'

Mysha bent down and retrieved Jaap's discarded cigarette butt, then put it to her nose and sniffed, play-acting, twitching her nose like a bunny rabbit. 'Spent lust,' she said. 'Incipient regret. Come the evening, he will be in need of comfort and reassurance.' She made to put the cigarette butt in her mouth, as if she wanted to eat it, or at least lick it. Lieve did not respond, and Mysha gave up on the charade. 'Oh, don't be so bloody moral, Lieve. Nothing's going to happen, I've already told you. And even if it did, no one would get hurt. Except you, perhaps.' Mysha dropped the cigarette back on the floor. 'You might. If you're feeling a little bit *jealous*?'

Lieve said nothing again.

What she wanted to say, was that it wasn't about being moral; it was a question of self-respect, and common sense. If Mysha did sleep with him, they'd get found out. There was no way someone like her could keep something like that a secret. She might not get kicked out of university, but Jaap would lose his job. It would be a move of irredeemable idiocy on his part.

They started walking back towards the university.

If you're going to sleep with a student, she didn't say, don't sleep with the stupid, pretty one. That would be a betrayal of the idea that sex and intelligence were in any way linked.

Fucking or no fucking, the exchange was clear, to her, and had been, in some form, from the first time she had stepped into a classroom. To sleep with Mysha would be a desecration of the unspoken, unformulated contract not between teacher and pupil, but between knowledge and the world.

'International business greetings,' Mysha said. This time her voice was mimicking Lieve's, and Lieve flushed to hear it. 'So pleased to meet you. Classic fricative transferral.' She opened and closed her mouth, and flapped her hands. Lieve didn't think she looked or sounded anything like that, but still it hurt. It was at times like this Lieve didn't see the point of being friends with Mysha, other than that she was really the only friend she had.

She stopped, so abruptly that the person behind them knocked into Mysha, and had to step around them.

'What?' Mysha said.

'Stop being such a bitch, Mysha.'

'I'm not the one being a bitch. You, getting all up everyone's arse with your international business greetings, you're the bitch. It's pathetic, listening to you two talk to each other. You're the one with your tongue out for him, not me.'

'Oh, fuck off.'

'What?'

'You don't know what you're talking about. You're just saying any old crap. Listen to yourself, Mysh.'

'No, you're the one who needs to listen to yourself. Because I've listened to it for long enough, and I'm sick of it. Jennifer Thursley, oh yes. She's so super-smart. Yes, Jaap. Yes, she is. Just like me. Just like you. We're all so super-smart. Good doggy. Pant pant, loll loll.'

Mysha was avoiding her gaze. People still moved around

them on the pavement. They'd been here before, or places like it – to do with Mysha's now ex-boyfriend, Greg, nearly as old as Jaap, and married, not that that had had anything to do with it. And then to do with her work, her bizarrely reactionary politics, considering the fact she was a second-generation immigrant and had dealt with her fair share of racism. Her snide comments about the woman in their cohort with autism, the two gay men. Her, in Lieve's eyes, general flakiness.

There was a moment between them, when Mysha, face somewhat askance, seemed to be wanting Lieve to say something to close the gap, to hold out an olive branch, and so allow her to apologise. But the moment didn't last, or else Lieve couldn't find it in herself to do it. So the moment ended. She would do it, sooner or later, she always did. If it happened later today, before or after their papers, she might be able to stop her friend from trying to sleep with their supervisor. But just now it wasn't on the cards. She wouldn't be the one to make the first move.

So Mysha went. See you later, they both said, avoiding each other's eyes.

Lieve looked around herself. A bar. A sandwich shop. A clothes store, with male mannequins standing in the window, in torn and patched jeans and zip-heavy leather jackets. She took a step out of the general flow of people towards the window, and leaned her forehead on the glass, letting the front of her woollen hat ride up so she could feel of the cold of it on her skin. She let herself listen to the movement of people past her, the words coming in fast-perishing snatches, in Dutch, French, American, Japanese. She was aware she must look odd, leaned against the window

like that, and aware, too, that she must look like the odd-
ness was intended, as if she was broadcasting her fragility,
her closeness to despair. She took a breath, and another, and
rolled herself sideways, from front to back, so she was now
leaning against a portion of wall next to the shop window.
People went past, and no one paid her any attention. And
that was alright.

She got out her phone and slipped off her gloves.
Nothing from Mysha, though she didn't expect it, not yet.
She opened her browser and searched for Jennifer Thursley.

Jenny had her phone out as she walked, and her glance
skipped with her steps from screen to street, street to
screen, looking up to check she wasn't about to walk right
into someone, looking down to see where she was. She considered what it might be that she reminded herself of, with
the phone held loose in her hand like that, her hand held
out in front of her. It was water dowsing, she realised. It was
as if she was dowsing for water.

She felt the prickle of heat under her dress as she walked.
It would be so good to have a bicycle, she thought. She
imagined herself passing through these streets up on a
saddle, elegant, effortless, erect. She came to a junction.
Across the street, behind a long rack thick with cycles was
an advertising billboard, a single poster in a vertical plastic
frame. She was seeing it at an angle, but something about
the image held her attention. She crossed over and stood
in front of it. It was an advertisement for the Rijksmuseum,
showing the image of a painting: a dark interior, five figures
around a table. All men, all wearing stiff wide cavalier hats,

and with lace collars and cuffs on their black jackets. That classic Dutch trick – it was Rembrandt, she saw – of having some of the characters turn towards the painter, as if caught in a moment, just breaking their pose.

The main figure, the one on the left, was looking down at the table, and had a finger set stiffly, proprietorially, on some pieces of paper laid out there. Another man, behind him, had a foot up on a chair, and was smiling out of the frame, as if on the point of making a satirical comment. Another man looked at the first man; another, on the right, was regarding the fifth figure, who was stood at the centre of the table. This man seemed less concretely painted in, as if unfinished, or as if only just emerging out of the many shadows. He wasn't wearing a hat; his head was indistinct and bare. He too was looking out at the painter, or the viewer, warily, as if he'd just caught sight of them.

It was just a painting. There were thousands like it. It was probably only famous because it was a Rembrandt, and why was Rembrandt was famous any more, other than for his self-portraits, and perhaps that one of his wife standing in a river in a nightshirt?

Jenny closed her eyes and breathed through her nose, imagining herself breathing the clear, cold air of the city. It reminded her of something – and not just Jaap's friend's painting, the painting in the room. She pictured the image. She opened her eyes and looked at it, closed her eyes again and saw it.

It was the table at breakfast.

Yes, when she looked again, she saw it. How the position of the people, and the geometry of their distinct and separate glances, all lived within the same plane, just as had been presented to her, that morning, in the view into the hotel dining room. Someone walked between her and the poster, pushing a buggy, blocking her view for a moment. The image was a reminder of the ignorance that had lurked inside her, that morning, unknown, malignant. And of the other ignorances that dwelt inside her, even now, all of them. All the things she didn't know, that she should. One of which would, in the end, be the thing that killed her. We can only move forward.

She had to finish her speech. That was an obstacle in the road. There were sudden shrieking bird calls and the beeps of a pedestrian crossing and a blown gust of conversation as people crossed the road behind her, all their words, thank Christ, entirely incomprehensible. If she had heard so much as a phrase, a word, in English, she would have screamed. She blinked her eyes and realised they had the beginning of tears in them. She thought of Frankie, at breakfast; Frankie at lunch. She thought of Leonard. He was here, in her reach, a person from her past life that could, remarkably, be grappled back to her, though to what purpose she could not think. Frankie, too. Frankie, whom she had loved, and left. Leonard, who had reached for her, and whom she had sidestepped. We can only move forward. That is the damnable thing. Whichever way we turn, we can only move in one direction.

She knuckled her eyes to clear them and stepped closer to the poster. It astonished her how open to interpretation the image was. How ready it was to be read, and how variously. Was it this, she thought: after all this time, all these years immersing herself in one medium, the stately parade of words in text and context, she was now presented with the suggestion that she had taken a wrong course. She was not a verbal person after all, but visual. She'd been making the wrong decisions, all along. She felt dazed, gutted, as if a layer of radical uncertainty had settled atop her tiredness, as if the world was trying to jog her into a terrible, decisive act. The decisive act was what she needed, the leap from the bungee platform, but when only one act was the right one, how did you know which one it was?

She turned from the poster, as in panic or fear. She had to go back to the hotel. There was so little time, perhaps already too little. She started walking, then broke into a trot, and looked behind herself as she made to cross the road, but pulled back in time to let a phalanx of bicycles pass. She felt herself spin, like litter in an eddy. She looked about herself. Across the road there was a coffee shop, a tattoo parlour, a hairdressing salon. This last seemed to offer some form of welcome, of safety. She shook her head at herself. This, after all, was the kind of thing she was good at, something entirely characteristic. Not to go to the conference, because she had to finish her speech. Not finish her speech because she fancied a haircut.

She crossed, looking carefully left and right, and looked in at the window. There seemed to be no customers inside. Someone who must have been the stylist was talking to the receptionist. She looked efficient, effective. She seemed ready to have someone throw herself on her mercy.

Jenny pushed open the door.

'Hi.'

'Hi. Sorry, do you speak English?'

'Of course.' Her head on one side, amused. 'How can I help?'

Jenny was surprised to find that she was again on the verge of tears.

'Is everything OK?'

'Yes, absolutely. Sorry, I'm just very tired. I flew in yesterday, I mean this morning, and I feel like...'

'You feel like you want a haircut?'

'Yes.'

'Or just wash and dry?'

'No, a haircut. Yes, please. That would be lovely. Sorry, I feel like I'm being stupid.'

'Not at all.'

The stylist took her coat and steered her to a seat. She was grateful for the speed of it, the sensibleness of it. She accepted the offer of a herbal tea, whether or not she would drink it.

'What shall we do then?' said the stylist, who introduced herself as Nienke. Nienke's hands were in her hair, where Jaap's had been. But quicker, defter, more sure of themselves.

She brushed it out, assessing its length and consistency. 'What are you thinking?'

Already Jenny felt the idiocy of it, the sheer unpardonable narcissism of doing this here, now. Her reflection seemed to stare her down.

'Well, actually, I think I want it all cut off.'

Jenny moved her hands about her head, miming perhaps the action of the scissors, or the shape of the hair when it was done. The words to describe what she wanted were there in her head, but she couldn't bring herself to say them. She didn't know if they would work, couldn't trust them to have the desired effect. Language falls apart when you so much as look at it. Eight trapdoors in every sentence.

'All off?' The stylist mimicked her gesture, sketching the outline of the as-yet non-existent hairdo. She had changed her voice, was speaking with a foreign accent – something foreign to both English and Dutch.

Jenny looked confusedly at her in the mirror.

She spoke again, accentuating the playfulness of voice and gesture. 'All off? Like in Roman Holiday? The film? Here?' She pulled Jenny's hair out straight and laid the blades of the scissors against it near the bottom, a look of comic horror on her face. 'Here? Here?' Shifting the implement up a centimetre at a time.

'Yes. All off,' said Jenny, half-changing her voice, too, trying, she supposed, to sound like Audrey Hepburn, although she had no real idea what that might sound like. A breathy nonsense.

'You know the film?'

'Of course.'

'I love it when people come in and ask for this,' said Nienke. 'It makes my day. It is the mark of a courageous person.'

Jenny nodded. She didn't feel courageous. 'All off,' she said again. Did this mean she was going to be made to look like Audrey Hepburn?

The washing and cutting passed as if in a dream. The close-range assault of the water from the shower head, the deep luxury of the shampooing, the slow urgent press of the fingers on her scalp, that told her she was a body, that she had bones beneath the skin. And then the warm towelling to bring her round. There was music playing in the salon, a French chansonnière. Sat back in the stylist's chair, Jenny felt cocooned. She became passive, letting her head be tilted and pushed this way and that, as Nienke hummed to herself, talked about what she was doing, now in English, now in Dutch: the tiny gentle shoves and settings-in-place that meant she was entirely under someone else's control. Jenny avoided looking in the mirror. She avoided thinking. She may have dozed off. No one ever knows exactly how long a haircut takes, how long it takes for every shorn hank of hair to drift deliriously to the floor. It is a time out of time, a window snipped out of the day. Death, she thought, might be quite like having your hair done.

Then Nienke was blasting her hair with a handheld dryer, angling it this way and that. She fussed about her fringe, and brought out the little mirror to show her the back.

'How's that?' she said.

'I love it,' Jenny replied, but she was not looking at herself in the mirror; she refused to catch her own eye. In truth she wanted out. She was scared that already she was failing to live up to the new person she had been given the opportunity to become.

She raced through payment, barely registering what it cost. In any case you only really know a new haircut from the first glimpse in a shop window, or the dark, distorted mirror of a car window. The passing, uncommitted glance; the momentary effect, not the scaffolding.

She stepped outside and immediately felt the afternoon air on her skin. She walked past the tattoo parlour, the coffee shop. She ran her fingers over the cropped hairs on her nape. It pleased her to think that the hair that Jaap had had his hand in an hour ago was no longer attached to her, but was, even now, being swept up from the floor and binned, mixed in with other people's cuttings. The shorn-ness gave her the feeling of an animal fresh out of hibernation.

She would head back to the hotel and work on the speech. Once the speech was sorted, she could face Leonard. And once she had been able to face Leonard, she would be able to face Frankie. She smiled to think of it, of Frankie seeing her haircut. She pulled her bag up on her shoulder as she walked, and turned her head to clock her reflection, submerged in the dark of a window, then another window, and another, her view of herself coming at her like stills in a flip book, or zoetrope. Moving forward, with a new haircut, it was easier, she felt, to move forward in time through the rest of your life.

8

When she got to her room, Jenny went straight to the mirror in the bathroom and surveyed herself. The line and weight of the cut were good, in and of themselves, but as a whole the cut gave the impression of dilating her face, as if under a magnifying glass. Her ears and nose, having been waiting patiently for years in the wings, had stepped into the spotlight. Her mouth seemed more sensual than before, but unduly exposed, as if that sensuality would have to account for itself. She would have to repaint it, and redo her eyes as well, to suit the frame in which they now operated. She brushed flightily at the fringe, scared of undermining or dislodging it. Yes, it was a good cut, but traumatically so. She felt like the house owner who, on repainting the woodwork, sees just how filthy the walls are.

She had picked up a couple of bottles of beer in a small supermarket en route to the hotel. Coffee, she'd thought, would further agitate the already jittery action of her thoughts. Even now it felt as if someone was blowing through a comb and a piece of tissue paper inside her head, every thought distorted, buzzing like a bust speaker cone. She used her cigarette lighter to open one of the bottles, then went to the window and had a drink, watching to see what might be happening outside. There was another building opposite, but no one was sitting there in the window, on show, offering themselves up as a model of how life might best be lived. The beer made her feel potent, and impatient. Its effect, she knew, would be temporary at best. It was a wave she would have to catch when it came.

She opened her laptop and looked for something to work to. She settled on the Bach violin partitas, then tabbed across to Word. There, still in two separate documents, were what she had so far. In one, a 2,000-word speculative ramble through the subjunctive that had originally been intended for some journal or other, but had fallen by the wayside. In the other, the sketched beginnings of an address about Leonard, or to him, she hadn't fully worked out which – but written when he was, to all intents and purposes, still immortal, alive, undying. She scrolled through it, wincing at what she found. It was a collection of false starts, as if someone had gone about a field, putting down here and there the foundations for a house, but deciding each time that the ground or the aspect was not right, and had given up and moved on. It was as if all this had been written consciously absent of a guiding principle that would bring the speech as a whole into focus. She knew now what that guiding principle was.

She scrolled back to the top and began to write.

It gives me great pleasure and pride to address you all, here, today, on the occasion of this celebration of the life and work of Leonard Peters. I have known Leonard for twenty years. Some of you, I know

She went back and deleted 'life and'.

A celebration of the work of Leonard Peters

Work and career

Work and life

Life and work

It is a blessing to have Leonard with us, so that we can speak to him. Here in the room with us. It is a privilege to be able to speak to him, or in his hearing, of his work, and its impact on us. To reflect back to him his own generosity and ingenuity, his intelligence, the warmth of his intelligence.

She looked at the words on the screen and felt a spasm in her diaphragm, a brief repeated rhythm. It travelled up through her chest to set off something behind her eyes.

She thought, naturally, of her father. Her speech, in the crematorium, with its large windows looking out over the Berkshire countryside, the benign watercolour view designed to distract you from the thick ruched curtains on the wall opposite, through which the coffin would leave. Low-ceilinged, compared to a church. God not present. God not liking to stoop, perhaps. The chairs arranged in shallow curved rows, such that, even half-empty, the room would not seem so. She had stood at the plain wooden lectern and read her piece, that she had written on this same laptop, or on one like it. Afterwards, she had burned for shame at feeling pride in what she said, at accepting the compliments that people gave her. The easy pity available to those speaking as if to someone that, lying so close by, could neither hear nor respond.

By contrast, anything she said to Leonard, tomorrow,

would have the ring of a death sentence about it. She was subject to the abysmal etiquette that attends the dying. To even gesture towards the word leaves a gap where it might have been spoken. To say it was unthinkable. It as good as denies the dying life, while they still have it. It is to drop poison in their cup that, while they hold it, is theirs to season as they wish.

The beer at least was working. She drank some more, and let the intricate stitchwork of the violin prick and re-prick her thoughts. She nodded her head in short loops along with it. It was quick and precise as a sewing machine, but intuitive and responsive, too, like knitting: it gathered and pulled its themes together as it went, tightening and tying off one thread even as it began the next. This was her chance to speak truth to Leonard, truth of the good he had done, no matter his one idiocy, let us assume it was one. Among the cacophony of feedback that modern life insists we submit at every turn, the gratuitous word of praise or appreciation has the concentrated power of a block of autumn sunlight falling through a window.

She thought of the postcard she had found pushed under her office door, not so long ago, of a Japanese woodblock print from the LA County Museum, with a few sentences carefully inscribed on the back – carefully, and anonymously. Dr Thursley, this is just to say I'm really enjoying your seminars this semester. Something you wrote on one of my essays last year helped me through a specific dark moment. You are a genius and we all think you're great, but you have been a particular personal inspiration, too. Thank you.

She had stuck the card – the image was of people going cherry blossom-viewing – on her cork board, and then found herself watching her students when they came in for tutorials, for any sign of recognition. She had seen nothing, and perhaps that was for the best. The card did its job just the same. She put down her beer and set her fingers again on the keyboard, feeling for the distinctive pattern of her opening spread, knowing she would be ready to write when her fingers were.

It is hard to know how to categorise the act of teaching, she typed, when it takes place at university level, when it is hoped that we have moved beyond the idea that students are vessels simply waiting to be filled with knowledge. When I think of Leonard at work, teaching, strangely enough, when I think of myself, as a graduate student, in one of his seminars in Manchester in the 1990s, the drab furniture and drabber views of F corridor, I don't think of him facing me, us, the students. He only faced us when he was listening, specifically, to a question or statement directly addressed to him. In fact he tried to avoid the sense that any statements or questions made by students should be addressed to him. 'You,' he used to say, with an expansive sweep of the arm, 'are the Academy. Not me.'

When he spoke, he set himself at an angle to us, as if what he was saying was not intended for us in particular, but rather what he was saying was something he was sending past us, this stream of thoughts and words and theories, so that we might pick out of it what we wanted or needed. Or else he spoke to the whiteboard, standing with his pen pressed against it, waiting for someone to say something, himself or a student. Even if what was most often said was, 'Sir, I think that might be a permanent marker you're using there.'

She stopped to drink, and scroll back up and down

again. She thought about Leonard, and then she thought about Frankie. It was she, after all, who had been the greater teacher, despite the fact that she had never actually taken a class with her. No one teaches you all you know, of course they don't, but there will be someone from whom you learn the most – somehow, somewhere, a quantifiable fact. It was from Frankie that she had learned how to learn, how to want to learn, how to feel the patterning of your mind shift as your worldview changes. A teacher is someone who leads you to the world – a particular part of it – shows you the view, and then steps away. Teaching as gesture, as the simple act of indication. She thought of her father, dying, his ignorance compounded by incoherence, the way his eyes tracked the doctors and nurses around the ward, as if they could save him from what was coming. The fear with which he viewed the other patients, as if it was their fault he was here, as if mortality was a contagion.

She had talked through so much of her work with Frankie. In pubs and cafés and on the sofa in the Hove apartment, with the yucca plants and Xena poster and sea-gulls honking and wheezing outside on the roofs, but also in the kitchen, in the bath, in bed. Those odd fledgling half-thoughts and ghost theories that come last thing at night, when your guards are down, or that have been hovering insubstantially in your mind all day and need fixing down lest they be quietly reabsorbed into the brain while you sleep. Something she might have said to Frankie, or Frankie to her. She thought of the two of them sat side by side in bed reading. A hand held out for a pen, to annotate or under-line, then the pen passed back. That was what characterised their relationship, any true relationship: the idea that you are side-by-side, facing the same direction, not facing each other. And, yes, it encompassed both friendship and desire.

Lying awake in her bed in Oakland, she sometimes spoke her thoughts aloud. And it was Frankie she wanted to have next to her, in these moments, to have her hear her words, make them real. Or sometimes not even hear them. Frankie had a marvellous capacity for sleep, a gift for it, even. Jenny loved to listen to the sound of her breathing as it stepped down through the gears from sleepiness to the threshold of sleep to near-silence. She loved above all those moments when she didn't know if she was asleep or not, awake or not, lying there right next to her, head on her pillow. The breath let out and then, after a moment, reeled back in. The lips, forgetful; the lashes, with their slow uncertain semaphore. The things she said to her, then, were the most important things of all, because she could never be sure if they would be heard – or if heard, fully understood.

It was then that she could whisper to her her most secret words, then listen for the barely muttered response, impossible to interpret, coming from somewhere apart from waking life, on the other side of some kind of door.

She blinked herself back to the room. She woke the laptop screen, then flicked her fingers on the computer touchpad, sending her words whirling away downscreen until, too soon, she hit the top of the document and the page bounced to a stop. She checked her word count. She checked her watch. It was nearly four o'clock. She had more to say about teaching, she felt. Say the things that Frankie would say, if it were she up there, on stage.

There is an eros of teaching, she wrote, that has nothing to do with the dynamics of power.

An eros of teaching

An eros of the classroom

An eros of learning

There is an eros of learning that has nothing to do with power, that can exist in the classroom, or the seminar room, or the tutorial, that has nothing to do with power, let alone to do with sex. Learning is all about the growth of the self, and teaching is about enabling that growth. The teacher is invested in the person that the student is becoming, and the student wants to share a sense of that person with their teacher, to show what they have learned – for how do you test your growing self except by exposing it to love or blame? The same dynamic, in the parent-child relationship, is marked and reinforced by a hug or a cuddle or a kiss. Not so in the classroom. Yet there has got to be something more going on than just the mark scrawled at the bottom of the essay, or entered on the computer. The pleasure taken in the shared awareness of personal development, the shared joy of someone seeing their chosen self emerge: this is the gift of eros.

I love you, she wrote.

I love you

I love you

I love you

She wrote it a dozen times, and she didn't know who she was writing it to. To Frankie? Yes, of course, but she didn't know if she could say it to her. To Leonard? Yes, she could say it, tomorrow. To someone else? She felt like the cat in the box with the pellet of poison, of whom nobody knew the state – living or dead – until they opened the lid; of whom the state was said to be double – both living and dead –

while the box stayed closed.

But she was the cat, itself not knowing which it was. Waiting for the lid to lift.

I love you.

She could stand on the stage and say, explicitly, to Leonard – say it to him, direct the words to him – that she and everyone in the room loved him. He was dying, and he was loved. Was that all she needed to say? Just stand there and say that, and then return to her seat. It was what everyone wanted to hear, or perhaps what they wanted to see him hear, there in the room.

She stood and took her beer to the window, and drank. The sky was darkening, the sun was on the other side of the hotel, and it flashed on the windows opposite. She finished her beer, then put her hands to her head, forgetful of the hair that was gone. She paced the room, mouthing to herself the same refrain: I love you, I love you, I love you. Who do you love? she asked herself, and that became her refrain. Who do you love? Who do you love? Who do you love?

She opened the second beer. She went to the bathroom and sat on the toilet. She peed, and tipped up the bottle so she drank as she peed. Thus the world passes through us, she thought, unfillable vessels. What's the point in loving anyone if we cannot hold love? It passes through us like beer.

She sat slumped on the toilet seat. Tiredness welled up like tears. The bed called to her, but she knew she must not give in to it. The thought of Leonard was proof against that. Let her think of him, every time she flagged. Your time on Earth is not short, but it shortens. There is less ahead than there is behind, but though the direction of travel cannot be changed, the landscape can be altered. Love is a golden age that can come again.

She jolted upright, wondering if she had momentarily slept, then got herself back to sorts. 'Come on,' she said. 'Let's do this.' She sat herself back at the laptop, pressed play on the music again, and scrolled back up to the top.

Lieve scanned the seminar room. There were twenty or thirty people already there, chatting amongst themselves or checking their phones. The emotions tumbled over each other: relief – that anyone had come at all – followed swiftly by dismay, that there was no backing out now, and she would have to do it.

Jaap was talking with someone by the computer pedestal at the front, by the screen. He had his back to her. There was no Jennifer Thursley, so far as she could see. No Mysha, either. She put down her bag and coat and removed the things she'd need: memory stick and printed sheets. She arranged them, without thinking, on the table. She had done this dozens of times before, or things like it; yet it seemed like something was required of her, here, before which she baulked.

Mysha at least would be an encouraging presence. Lieve wished she were here. There were some other students she knew in the audience, and some of them came up to wish her good luck, but she had nothing to say back to them. Only Mysha's blind confidence seemed, just now, the needed thing.

She loitered, waiting for Jaap. Someone attached a microphone to her collar, and she fiddled with it for a minute or so. When he came to the end of his conversation and looked for her, she was right behind him, and she jumped, stupidly, from surprise.

'There you are,' he said, all efficiency.

'Look, Jaap. I just wanted to say...'

'Lieve.'

'No, this is important.'

He checked his watch and glanced at the room, but Lieve cut him off.

'I just wanted to say,' she said again. 'I mean, I wanted to apologise for earlier on. It was such a stupid thing to do.'

'Yes, it was,' he said. 'But it's done, and it's forgotten.' His voice was quiet and confiding. He lifted his hands and brought them gently down to rest on her shoulders. 'Just focus on your session. You're going to be great, I know. It's a good crowd. Dominique is here, and Mehmet. Jennifer Thursley couldn't make it, after all. She's had to go and' – he dropped his voice, so he was mouthing the words – 'finish her speech. But I'll introduce you later. Don't worry. About any of it.'

Again Lieve felt relief and something counter to it, that she couldn't name. Jennifer Thursley wasn't there, which was a good thing, because how awful would it be to do this with her there, in the front row, staring at her? But the fact that this was a good thing only showed up what an idiot she had been in the first place. This was her chance to have her ideas heard, to make a connection. To *kill it*.

'So,' Jaap said. 'Are you ready?'

He checked his watch. He looked relaxed, and that relaxed her.

'Yes.'

'Good, then.'

He clapped his hands for quiet, then introduced her. The room was quite full now, maybe forty or fifty people, and they applauded politely. She waited for him to take his seat, then began.

'Hi there, and thank you for coming. My name is Lieve Braam and I am a doctoral student here in the Linguistics Department at the University of Amsterdam.' She stole a glance at Jaap, in the front row. He had his legs crossed and was leaning sideways, hands clasped on his knee. 'Today, I will be presenting some of my research into the transnational aspects of business etiquette in the Indo-European languages. Which is, I promise you, more fun than it sounds. Before I start, I feel I should warn you that there will be audience participation. No pressure, but if you aren't in the mood for fun role-plays then now would be a good time to step out.'

She left a beat for appreciative amusement, of which they was some, at least.

'What I would like you to do, to start, is to turn to the person next to you and introduce yourself. Imagine that you are meeting for the first time. If you know the person next to you, then look around you for someone you don't know.'

Thank god, people did as she asked.

While they did so, she walked softly up the aisle running down the centre of the room, listening to people on each side. She had her hands clasped one over the other in front of her stomach, like her primary school teacher always did, Miss Janssens, her fingers locked over and under each other in tight symmetrical twinship. She caught a phrase here, a phrase there, repeating them to herself in her head to try to fix them in her memory. She listened as stilted greetings expanded into playful conversations.

She felt she was beginning to see how teaching itself could be a thrill, could carry a real emotional charge. To stand, when others were sitting. To be the focus of the room, but to be in control of that focus. To allow it to settle on oneself, or to redirect it, reflect it, sometimes even dissolve it, or diffuse it throughout the room, but be able to gather it back to yourself at any time. To be a good teacher meant being both passive and active. It did not mean to call up knowledge, but to generate the feeling for knowledge, and then to control that flow of feeling in the room, to be able to respond to and control the power of those feelings in other people.

She slowly walked back towards the front of the room.

'Now then,' she said, when she had their attention again. 'First of all, I hope you enjoyed meeting each other. That is partly what a conference like this is about, after all. But also, listening in, what quick points can I find? Firstly, most of you spoke English. This is to be expected. After all, many of you are British or American. I am speaking English, as is normal in the Dutch education system. Please, put your hand up if you introduced yourself in a language other than English.'

A few hands went up – maybe ten.

She thought of Miss Janssens, the way she behaved in the classroom. It was partly the clasped hands that came back to her, and the stillness that this signified. It was a pose reminiscent of a singer about to launch into a recital, while the hands themselves, the fingers folded over and under each other, seemed more like something from Zen Buddhism, or the crucible for a sacred flame.

At first Lieve, like all children, had thought that what

happened in the classroom was that they sat there, while Miss Janssens taught them, but in retrospect this seemed not to be the case. It was not that Miss Janssens instructed the children in her care, but that she organised their day so that learning would happen. The learning happened with something like magic. Miss Janssens stood at the white-board and wrote out sums, or spelled out words; she read them stories, as they sat cross-legged on the carpet; but the real learning happened when she had set them all a task and they were working on it, silently, six to a table, heads down, pencil hands aching and mouths tight with concen-tration. It was then that she walked softly between them, hands clasped before her, watching over them.

Learning dwelt in the schoolhouse, as God dwelt in the church next door, and Miss Janssens was in the school as the priest was in the church: not the fount of what would be found there, but its handmaiden, in some way its guarantor.

Standing at the front of the room, Lieve imagined herself as her old teacher. She saw how the eyes of the attendees rested on her, variously curious, ironical and inattentive, and saw in them the desire to be returned to the classroom, to a state not just of innocence, but of immanence, of read-iness to learn. She smiled at the thought that she could see in them – these people, her peers, many of them her seniors – what they couldn't yet see in themselves.

The thought then came back to her of Mysha giving her paper, the joke-thought of her grinding and gyrating like a stripper in a club as she laboured her points about vowel shifts and fronting in Germanic languages, tossing back her long hair, angling her shoulder, knee and hips in a fluid round of poses, running her hands over the sides of her breasts and down her flanks. The thought was delightful, and disastrous. Instantly the thought bled from Mysha to herself, and she imagined herself moving like that, imagined herself doing it now, turning her back on the audience and then half-turning back to face them, running a hand over her cheek and lip, pouting as she spoke. She might tip up her chin, might dip her knees and press her hands to the small of her back as she lowered herself. She thrilled at the ludicrous fact that she could think like this, quite blatantly, while all these people heard only her words – at the thinness of the membrane that kept our thoughts hidden from other people, that kept us from tipping over into our worst desires. It was a miracle, really, that such things as conferences, as linguistic departments, could even exist, with all these disastrous thoughts boiling around underneath them.

She clapped her hands.

'Thank you,' she said. 'I'll talk some more about these interactions in a moment, but first for the next section I need a volunteer. Could someone step forward, please. It's nothing scary, I promise.'

9

Jenny walked quick-march back to the conference building, feeling the first intimations of drunkenness flutter in her knees and the back of her head – as if there was a gap there for it, as if something inessential had been removed. The sun had dropped behind the tops of the houses, and she pulled her coat about her neck and ducked her bare cold head in penance. There were still people in the streets, but not the groups of students and schoolchildren of earlier: they were safely back in their coaches or hostels. What cyclists there were leaned into their work, committed to getting home; Jenny shared their sense of urgency. What before had been dread, for what she would say tomorrow, or how she would deal with Leonard, had resolved itself to a determination to find Frankie, and talk to her, properly. Find Leonard, too, and talk to him. But mostly, find Frankie. The speech was done, as done as it would ever be. That would be fine, if only she could sort everything else out.

The entrance to the university building was largely empty

now, but as she approached the conference suite she could hear sound from the auditorium, amplified speech. In the reception she found a team of catering staff readying the next stage of the evening. Some stood waiting, trays held slack by their sides, while others poured sparkling wine in flute glass after flute glass set out on the tables, freshly dressed with new white cloths. From the doors to the lecture theatre, which were open, Jenny could hear a voice, and then applause. More speaking, and more applause.

As if by chance she drifted to one of the tables, where she took a filled glass, impishly raising it in salute to the nearest server, and went to look in at one of the doors.

There on the stage was Jaap, her former lover for the length of a kiss, and a Dutch-looking man she didn't know. The man was talking about Jaap. Jaap stood, arms crossed, listening carefully. He looked immensely, unironically pleased with himself. Jenny scanned the room. Fewer people than before, but still at least a couple of hundred. There was Leonard, back in his seat in the front row. Frankie next to him, leaning in slightly towards him.

'So I am pleased to announce,' said the man, speaking slightly laboriously, 'the founding of a Chair in Historical Linguistics here at the University of Amsterdam, and that its first incumbent is to be Jaap Vos.'

Jenny rested herself against the doorjamb and watched him. More applause. Some wolf whistles, and a shouted comment in Dutch that drew laughter. She raised her glass in a private toast and drank.

The men shook hands, and a photographer crouched his way towards them across the stage, snapping and moving.

Jaap responded to the announcement, laughing at the

whoops and cheers from his students at the front, some of whom were making kowtowing gestures, or pumping the air like cheerleaders.

Jenny didn't particularly wish to hear what he would have to say at this juncture. She swapped her empty glass for a full one, then wandered over to the window by the courtyard and looked out, leaning in and blocking the light with her spare hand so she could see. Lit from below by angled lamps set in the ground, the low square hedges looked artificial, the statues rawly abstract. She had sat there that morning, trying to take in the news about Leonard. She was still trying to take it in, but the task was achievable, she thought. Things remained within her grasp.

Then people started to come out, and she positioned herself, as earlier, to spot and pick out Frankie, but she was overwhelmed by the flood of people, louder and quicker and moving in more complex patterns than before, and by the deft comprehensive response of the servers, who fanned out by the doors to catch them as they came and distribute their glasses of sparkling wine. Jenny retreated, scanning the crowd, but here suddenly was Andrea Owen bearing down on her, with a look on her face of confusion and – if Jenny read her right – amusement that involved her opening her eyes shockingly wide and retracting her chin into her neck.

Jenny stared back at her in an equal confusion, before it clicked.

'Oh, the hair?' she said. 'You mean the hair.'

'*Yes* the hair! You got your hair cut since this morning? That's... superb!'

Jenny shook her head yes. It occurred to her that this was a conversation she would have to have many more times over the rest of the evening, and tomorrow. Perhaps for the rest of her life. Getting your hair cut mid-conference was indeed the act of an attention-seeker, of someone who expected a remark from everyone she met. She looked around, but it was too late to think of escape. There was something about Andrea Owen, about her voice, or the way she deployed herself in space, that drew people to her, and already Jenny found they were half-surrounded.

She shook hands and kissed cheeks and repeated back names she immediately forgot, and laughed and batted away compliments – on her hair, on her work, on the speech she hadn't yet given – and gave compliments, herself, to be batted away in turn; it was dispiriting, and it was debilitating. She allowed herself to become part of the group, tilting her head to show attention.

She could see now how Leonard's death floated behind every conversation, or perhaps in front of it. You had to speak through it to reach the other person. It was never alluded to, but always entirely assumed. It was there in the wan swerve of people's smiles. It was there in the sad lift of their eyebrows. His death was the ghost at the feast.

Jaap's announcement, however, together with the booze, had lifted the volume and, seemingly, the oxygen level in the room. Jenny tried to keep an eye out for Frankie and Leonard, but neither was in evidence. She nodded and smiled, and agreed with everything that was said to her. She modestly placed her hand over her glass when a server came by with more sparkling wine, then coyly gave in to admonishments and lifted it off.

Andrea Owen revealed herself to Jenny as the kind of person who monopolised a conversation by making it not all about herself at all. She prodded people with the questions they should all be asking Jenny, and filled Jenny in on what everyone else had been doing. She seemed to want to act, herself, as an entire social network, building connections and facilitating dialogue and self-disclosure, and all the time gleaning some dividend for this in a way that wasn't, to its users, entirely transparent. Every person who joined the group was, somehow – and at a level that just about avoided rudeness – invited to marvel at Jenny's hair, and at the fact she had transformed herself so gloriously in the middle of an international conference. And somehow that marvel seemed to speak in part to Andrea Owen.

Jenny began to hate her hair.

She had just plucked up the courage to tear herself away, draining her glass as pretext, when Andrea Owen gave an O of exclamation and put her hand on Jenny's wrist.

'Jenny! Lieve. You've just got to meet Lieve, if you haven't met her. Have you met her?'

Jenny doubted she had.

Lieve was a woman maybe ten years younger than Jenny. Her hair was cropped close to her head, almost Russian-looking, or like a marine's. She wore tailored slacks, and a tank top, with the narrow collars of her shirt just poking above the round neckline. She had a piercing in her nose, and a stud and a ring in the lobe of her ear, but for all that she was more elegant than punky.

Jenny put her hand out and said hello, but the response she got was unexpected.

Lieve did put her hand out to place it in Jenny's, but she did it very slowly, as if under some kind of compulsion. Her look was, bizarrely, one of dismay and bewilderment, and for once it didn't seem likely that this was down solely to Jenny's hair, though she too was eying it, in passing.

'Lieve, yes?' Jenny said, trying not to sound condescending, for the poor woman looked ready to cry, or run. 'Am I saying that right?'

'Sure,' she said, in a manner suggested that nothing was less sure.

'You haven't met, then?' said Andrea Owen.

'No,' they both said, and Jenny saw that the woman was blushing, her eyes wide and rimmed with moisture. She tried to recall her name, but it had already gone, tumbled out of the back of her head like a table tennis ball bouncing out of a bowl.

'Lieve gave a wonderful paper on business linguistics this afternoon that used some of your work on communications theory. Just wonderful. You weren't there, I don't think.'

Lieve, Jenny told herself, digging a nail into her palm to fix the name: Lieve – then she remembered. This was Jaap's student.

'Oh god, yes. No. I'm so sorry I missed it,' she said. 'Jaap Vos – your supervisor, right? – mentioned it to me.'

'She had some of us up at the front of the room,' said Andrea Owen, 'doing role play. Such fun.'

'That sounds fascinating. You must email me a copy of the paper.'

'Of course,' said Lieve.

Again, this muted, almost churlish response wasn't what Jenny expected. Not the usual queasiness of a student tongue-tied in the presence of a superior.

Lieve took back her hand and ran it in an involuntary, self-conscious pass over her head. The strands of hair made gorgeous whorl-like patterns across her skull, like iron filings caught in a magnetic field. It occurred to Jenny that hair that short would need regular attention. She wondered if she went to a salon to have it done, or if she did it herself, or had someone who would do it for her. Jenny resisted the urge to mimic the gesture, to touch her own hair, her own newly exposed skin.

'I'm really very pleased to meet you, Doctor Thursley.'

Lieve seemed to have pulled herself together.

'Jenny, please,' Jenny said.

'Of course, thank you. What I mean to say is, your work has been very influential on my own PhD. It's opened up all different kinds of avenues. It really made me rethink what I was trying to do.' Her voice deepened as she got herself back on track. 'I was in business before I came to study here, in corporate communications, and, well, your research kind of linked those two worlds for me. It was very important for me, at the time.' She gave a nod of affirmation, as if she had succeeded in saying what she had intended. She looked relieved.

'I'm glad. Thank you. That's lovely to hear.'

'Of course, it was Jaap who introduced me to your work…'

And it was then, as Lieve's sentence kind of crumpled under her, for she got no further than that, that Jenny realised more precisely who she was. The way she had said Jaap Vos's name had had a kind of challenge to it, almost a lasciviousness. It was on that that she had faltered. This, Jenny realised, was one of the women by the canal, outside the house. The two women that Jaap had chased after and remonstrated with. They had somehow been following them: Jaap, or her, like a couple of terrible spies.

Jenny felt her expression change as the knowledge

bloomed in her features. She was grinning, she couldn't help it. The woman – Lieve – looked away and began, again, to blush. When she looked back it was with an angry pout that Jenny recognised, for it was one she had used often enough herself in her time. Oh you silly, Jenny wanted to say. This was not judgement. If anything, this was complicity, in whatever prank she – they – had tried to pull.

Andrea Owen looked between them, a smile hovering about her lips that she did not feel able to commit to. The other people in the group looked more confused still; they were confused by Andrea Owen's confusion, bless them, out of sheer loyalty.

A server with a tray of drinks passed by, and Jenny reached out to set down her empty glass. She took two new ones and passed one to Lieve, who took it reluctantly, as if against her better judgment.

'So,' she said, and she tried to make her words sound convivial, intimate, even mischievous. 'Tell me about Jaap Vos. About *Professor* Vos. He seems like an interesting person.'

'Ah, well. Of course, he's my supervisor, so I have only good things to say about him.'

Her voice was that of someone testing the water, provisionally extending their trust.

'So, tell me some of the good things.'

'Well, he's super-smart. I mean he's a really clever guy. A good teacher. He understands what I'm trying to do. He takes it seriously. He doesn't try to take over your work. He lets you get on with it.'

Andrea Owen was nodding along. She seemed relieved they had found solid ground. Jenny sipped her drink and looked over the rim of it at Lieve; she flicked up her eyebrows to indicate she should continue.

'I don't know what else to say,' she said. 'He's... funny? He's a good dresser. But he's got a terrible taste in music.' She seemed to be observing Jenny as she talked, watching for her reaction. 'And – but perhaps you know – he's a terrible, terrible dancer.'

'Well, no, I don't, as it happens,' Jenny said, mildly taken aback.

She took the opportunity to check the room. When she did, she found herself looking directly at and being looked at by none other than Jaap Vos, who was standing about three groups away. He waved, and made some vague hand gesture, mouthing something she couldn't understand. She lifted a hand in response, she hoped noncommittally, but either it wasn't noncommittal enough, or else its degree of noncommitment made no difference, for he made his way over towards them, slipping himself sideways between the intermediate groups.

It was only when he got to their group, however, that he saw that Lieve was part of it. Jenny watched him try to parse the situation – the quick shuttling flurry of eye movement, the whirring of the cogs to gauge who knew what and what was known.

'Ah, so you've met Lieve at last,' he said. 'Good.'

To hear it, nothing sounded less good. 'Yes, I have,' Jenny said.

'Good. I'm glad.' He sounded like someone who wanted to sound like they were in full possession of the facts. 'And' – he leaned back, as if to appraise her from afar – 'You've had your hair cut, I see.'

'I have. Well spotted.'

'It looks' – he gestured with his hands, as if trying to conjure the right word – 'splendid. Congratulations!'

'Well, congratulations to you.'

She raised her glass, and the others joined in, toasting him.

Jaap bowed his head in faux-modesty. 'Thank you. It feels like a huge honour. It's been incredibly hard having to keep quiet about it.'

He sneaked a glance at Lieve. Lieve, too, Jenny noticed, was spending as much time observing her and Jaap as Jaap was her and Lieve. She wondered if they were sleeping together: the thought didn't seem impossible, based on what little she knew of Jaap. She wanted to shake her head, like a dog shakes itself dry after a swim, to dislodge all these unfinished thoughts. It was Frankie and Leonard she had to concentrate on, not these two. Whatever games they were involved in were not her concern. The wine, on top of the beer, and the jet lag, was increasing its toll. She could feel it creeping up on her.

Now it was Andrea Owen who spoke. 'Lieve here was just telling us what a good dancer you are, Jaap,' she said.

Lieve looked into her glass, ashamed.

'Oh, don't embarrass her, please,' Jaap replied. He put his hand on Lieve's shoulder. 'In fact, she is the one who is the good dancer. I've seen her dance, and she puts us old bastards to shame. And I imagine Jenny can tear up the dance floor with the best of them.' He put his other hand on Jenny's elbow, playfully patriarchal, as if the irony could excuse the awfulness of the gesture. She raised her eyebrows at Lieve to show surprise – not at what he said, but that he said it – and Lieve kind of goggled her eyes in response.

'Tonight, however, all will be made clear,' Jaap said, oblivious. 'For tonight there will be dancing.' He took back his touch from them both – and you could read that touch in two ways, Jenny thought: either as a statement of strength and ownership on his part, or as one that formed secret connections through him, without his knowledge. He gave a little jig, pumping his fists and raising his knees. A miniature joke of a dance. It seemed at once self-mocking and strategic, setting firmly on one side the question of whether he was actually any good at dancing.

Andrea Owen clapped her hands with glee.

Lieve looked embarrassed, but laughed and shook her head.

Jenny leaned in to Lieve. 'Very nice to meet you,' she said. She held out her hand again, and this time the younger woman took it with no hesitation. The hand was cool, and poised, and Jenny had to resist the urge to grip it more tightly, to see what would happen if she did. 'Perhaps we can speak later. I'd like to hear more about your paper.' Lieve nodded, smiled. 'But now I should go. There's someone I need to talk to.'

She got another glass, more for disguise than need, and moved around the edge of the room, looking. It was filled out with people, more than a hundred, certainly. It had become vitally important to find Frankie. She needed to talk to her. The words were caught in her chest, like heartburn. Until she had talked with Frankie her life was essentially in stasis.

At one point, as she moved and looked, she found that she was quite close to Leonard, who was standing leaning on a chair back, and dipping his head to hear someone talk, but she couldn't speak to Leonard until she had spoken with Frankie. She went up on tip-toe for a better view, and nearly lost her footing. Someone put out their hand to steady her. She smiled her thanks and put down her glass on a nearby table. She mustn't drink too much, she told herself, knowing full well that she wasn't listening.

In the end they came upon each other entirely by chance. A couple talking moved out of the way and there they were, face to face.

Frankie gave a great bark of surprise and put her hand to her mouth.

'Good god.'

'What?'

She shrieked. 'Jenny. You've... what have you done?'

'You don't like it?'

'I *love* it! You're like your own younger sister. It's adorable.'

Frankie reached out and ran her fingers across Jenny's fringe, brushing it in little movements flat across her forehead. Jenny moved her head gently to the side, to let her feel, and see, more. She felt the soft blunt ends of Frankie's fingers near her skin; the new hairs prickled on her nape. The memory of being in the salon chair rose and settled about her, the sense of giving herself over to someone else's care.

'Adorable, just adorable.' Frankie took back her hand. 'Did Jaap Vos do it? Is he a stylist on top of his other various talents?'

'Ha, no. It was a spur of the moment thing.'

'Well: well done. It's lovely. How are you bearing up, anyway? Have you spoken to Leonard yet?'

'No.'

This earned her a dubious glance. 'Jenny...'

'Look, can we get a drink?'

'Of course. So then,' said Frankie, as they moved through the throng. 'Jaap Vos. Tell me about your date.'

'If you want to call it that.'

'You meet for a coffee. Three hours later, he's a Professor, and you have a new haircut. I'm intrigued. Is there anything else I should know?'

'It was interesting,' Jenny said. 'He showed me a room with a painting in it.' The room with the painting was not long ago, but she couldn't fix it in her memory. Not with the alcohol pounding in her head like water against a dam wall. 'He made love to me.'

'You speak archaically, of course.'

'It was an archaic moment. As passes go, it was thoughtful, and apposite. It was real, I give him that at least.' She shrugged. 'But in any case, it's done with.'

She snatched a glance at Frankie, to see how she had taken this, but she was leaning to take a canapé from the tray of a passing waiter. Jenny followed suit. It was a blini with a thick smudge of sour cream and something herby. She popped it into her mouth, then turned with the waiter as he continued past them and took two more.

Frankie was nodding with overt appreciation. 'These are *good*,' she said.

'They're like sweets,' Jenny said, wanting to be clever, wanting to be loved.

'Sweets.'

Jenny washed the cakelet down with sparkling wine, juggling the others so they rested safely in her palm. Desperation was making her hands sweat.

'Each individual one is only really pleasurable to eat insofar as it posits the pleasurableness of the next one. Have one.' She held her hand out to Frankie, who declined. 'Pleasure deferred, infinitely, or as close as. Which means, I suppose, that it's only ever the last one that truly tastes good.' She put another blini in her mouth.

'By which time you'd feel too sick to enjoy it.'

'Exactly.' Spoken, deliberately, through the half-chewed mess of food: as a provocation. You see, she wanted to tell Frankie, or wanted Frankie to know: this is how we were. We can be like this again. But Frankie broke off and reached into her bag. She brought out her phone and swiped the screen.

Jenny saw there was a text.

'Leonard,' Frankie said, and a spasm of concern briefly etched her face. 'Come on,' she said, catching Jenny by the elbow, coaxing her. 'Come and talk to him.' When she wanted to, Frankie could sound as deeply compelling, as deeply true, as a Jesus from a Bach Passion. She was operatic in her tendency. 'You've got to talk to him. This is getting silly.'

Jenny felt the panic rise again. As if the thing, after all, *could* be contagious.

'I know. But not now.' Not until I've spoken to you, she didn't say. Don't leave me, she didn't say. I love you, she didn't say.

'He gets tired easily. You mustn't leave it too late.'

'I know,' she said. Stay with me now, she didn't say. Don't let me leave it too late, she didn't say.

'I mean it.' Frankie rubbed her arm. She felt her hand through the knit of her dress, how the fabric met and recognised her touch, the cool press of it. Frankie brushed again at her hair, there at the side of her ear. 'Don't leave it too late.'

But the thing that she thought was: what if it is too late, now, already?

Lieve sat outside on a stone bench, smoking. She didn't have her coat, and it was properly cold now. The dark sky above the courtyard had clouded over; the grey clouds were tinged yellow on the underneath, in stripes, like a running kit. The bench was tucked behind a sculpture, so she was hidden from the windows of the conference reception area. She thumbed through her phone. She thought about Jenny Thursley, and Jaap. It unnerved her to think that she couldn't work out what their relationship was. To disappear into a house like that for half an hour, or longer – that wasn't even Jaap's own home, it transpired – did make it look like an assignation, but there was nothing in their interaction to suggest erotic charge. Though that could mean nothing. Despite what Mysha said, Lieve didn't think sexual entanglement was visible on the exterior. People who shagged in secret most likely got good at dissembling in public. She had long ago shed the habit of thinking that any recent orgasm would be evident in her face.

And then to see her, Jenny Thursley, with her hair cut. She tried to remember how it had looked before. It had been long, but done up on the top of her head. She Googled her again, but the only images of her online – dull posed head-shots linked to her academic profile – looked old, and made her look older than she remembered her. She drew on her cigarette. What did she look like now? She had trouble visualising her. There was a definite, almost defiant fringe.

At the back, all gone. But that fringe, flicking boyishly across her forehead. She opened her camera app, switched it to front camera and regarded herself. In the dark of the court-yard she was indistinct, a blurred mash of pixels in greys and beige browns.

She messaged Mysha.

Where are you? Are you still here? Lx

She scrolled up through the conversation, and back down again: nothing. She opened her bag and dropped the phone in, next to her notebook. She thought back to her scribbled words of that morning: the way social media concertinaed together action and reflection, text and inter-pretation, collapsing idea and reality, emotion and response into one virtual space. What had felt like intelligent insight then now felt queasily personal. The very last thing Lieve wanted to know was what she thought or might think about the choices surrounding her, crowding in on her from the immediate future and past. She dropped her cigarette end and twisted it into the gravel. A ping came from the bag.

It was Mysha: Yes I'm here. Are you here? Are you drunk yet? I'm drunk I think. Where are you? Are you ALONE?

Lieve replied: No not drunk. Yes alone.

You surprise me. I saw you getting your congratulations in early. I'm sure you'll be very happy.

Don't be daft, Lieve typed. That's not what

She backspaced, then tried again: Haha. Forget it. He doesn't want to fuck me and I don't want to fuck him. You go right ahead. She tapped send, heard the whoosh, and saw the words slip inside their balloon and slide upscreen. Looked at the screen, and felt her stomach drop. What a stupid thing that was to write.

The message came back: Well, if you say so. Don't say I didn't give you first dibs. And a smiley with lolling tongue, a banana, a peach, fireworks.

She sat back on the bench so she was leaning against the sculpture, and closed her eyes. Mysha was an idiot, but to be outfoxed by an idiot was intolerable. The idea that Mysha might – purposefully or not – bounce her into a stupidity greater than she herself was capable of shocked her. The conference had felt like a critical moment in her career, but that moment seemed to be slipping away from her, or rather, it had tilted, and was sliding her towards something else, something entirely unexpected and not to be thought of.

Jenny had watched Frankie go, wishing she could go with her, and hating herself for not going. She felt like a coward. She wasn't ready to talk to Leonard, even though that was what she knew she had to do. His life and his work. His life and work. She knew what she wanted to say. He was dying, and that was fine because he was loved and respected. She knew she could say it. Or rather, she would know if she would be able to say it when she looked him the face. She was ready to do that. Yet she hadn't done it.

She had drunk more sparkling wine and gobbled down more canapés to still the churn in her gut. Later, they had been moved down a corridor that skirted the formal court-yard, with its shrubs and statues, and through a different set of double doors into a large room that was somehow suddenly in an older part of the university building, with wood panelling and heavy curtains hanging in the tall leaded windows. There was food laid out on tables running along two walls, with other, round tables set out to sit and eat at, though people were still too full of talk and energy to settle.

Jenny stood against the back wall, half-leaning with a glass of what was now white wine, observing. She told herself she was observing. Every time she looked around there were more people, and, every time, the people were talking louder. Louder as they queued. Louder as they took food. Louder as they stood, plate in hand, kept from sitting and eating by the urgent need to keep talking, to keep the volume levels high.

She saw how gestures grew in expansiveness. People were quicker to laugh, quicker to agree. It was as if they knew that if they all stopped talking and listening and agreeing and answering and suggesting, even just for a second, the plates and glasses, the food and drink in all their myriad combinations, like something from a morality play, would all disappear.

They were being orchestrated, Jenny thought, or rather they were being choreographed. The wine and canapés had been the overture, and the pace at which these had been circulated gave the guests the measure by which they, themselves, should move and mingle, once they moved on to this new room, for the second movement. And in moving like this, in keeping the room in motion, they were behaving like individual semantic units, mimicking the action of language itself, that acquires meaning only in exchange. Together they formed a conversation that, stuck inside it, they could not understand.

On a low raised area at the end of the room a string quartet had set itself up. They played as people ate; perhaps it aided the digestion. Jenny took her wine and a plate of food and sat near them to watch. They were young – students, presumably: adorable in their tuxes and gowns, and in their commitment to the music. Even as they played on their instruments, they performed the playing of them. Every draw of the bow, every toss of the cellist's long, light-as-air hair. The way their shifting postures on their four chairs presented an intricate dance, passing the thread of the music between them like an unravelling, tangling ball of wool between kittens. She thought about movement and stasis. About the way the instruments conversed, each to each. The lines that could be drawn between them. The violin music she had listened to in the hotel had been different: the sound of one mind following its thought just as far as it could go. This music was like the story of a series of relationships. Not one mind, but four. Four souls in flux and debate. She drank her wine and waited for Frankie and Leonard to come back in.

Then she saw Leonard, sat at a table. He was talking with Jaap. In his physical exhaustion he looked both limp and strung out tight enough to snap. He looked unequal to the moment, unequal even to the glass of beer at his elbow. Jenny could imagine how much he would hate all this: the noise, the surface agitation, the endless lines of people to see, talk to, recognise. Was this what a Festschrift was, then? Company men got a carriage clock. Professors got eulogies and poached salmon and Dvorak played by students from the College of Music?

She accepted with a dignified tilt of the head a top-up of her glass from a waiter. She didn't mean eulogies, there was another word, something that didn't imply the person being praised was already dead and buried. And again the thought of the talk she would have to give, tomorrow, assaulted her. What she had originally written was trash, but it was honest trash, written for a living person. Anything she wrote now, or anything she spoke, would be hedged about with the worst kind of mawkishness, as if it came with its own background music, like a schmaltzy film unsure of its own power to engage.

And yet that was her job. To stand up in front of everyone and tell them the news that they already knew. That Leonard had done all of that work – his life, his career – and now here he was. But how else are you supposed to express your admiration? What are the options? What is permitted?

She considered Jaap again. His – seemingly – genuine response to her work struck her more each time she thought of him, or it. His emails, that amounted to a personal commentary on what had seemed to her the driest of academic papers, now seemed to turn them into something more than that, something worth reading, worth having written. In showing Jenny her own work in a new and kindly light, Jaap was entering into an exchange with her thoughts and ideas that was powerful enough to cross the mind-body membrane. Was that not the dynamic underlying every academic exchange? The corridors, the journals, were full of it. Conferences were simply where what was latent became manifest.

We speak of admiration, respect, friendship. But if the expression of that admiration takes the form of the sexual, who's to say that's not appropriate? The sexual gesture speaks to something that just cannot be conveyed by keynote address, nor by any words spoken with rented glass of wine in hand. Even a hug can't do it, the social act that mimics the sexual one so brazenly, and insidiously. The bliss of contact, the shock of boundaries overstepped. The breadth of physical coverage, as it happens. The brevity of it, when it's over.

She swung her gaze back to Leonard, and the thought arose, and she dwelt on it, with a miserable kind of exultation – inserting it like the point of an unbended paperclip under the skin of her vanity – that she might actually offer herself, now, in a belated show of esteem, or gratitude, or penance.

The string quartet continued, undaunted, attacking their polkas and polonaises with something approaching righteous indignation.

There's something I want to tell you, she might say, but I can't tell you it here.

Or, I think we have some unfinished business, Leonard.

What nonsense. She wouldn't, couldn't, say that, any more than she could clamp her mouth on his, take him by the tie and lead him, strutting like a whore, from the room. These were goads, small injuries perpetrated upon herself, to bring herself to herself, put herself in her place, distract herself from the fact that in a few hours she would be standing up in front of everyone present and addressing them, addressing Leonard, and not knowing – not knowing in any manner or form – how she was to do it, how she should begin, let alone carry on and continue. What modulation of emotion was she supposed to apply to the words she had written for herself to speak; words that were, after all, not just to him and about him, but of him, from him, using him and his ideas, the bulk of his body of work, as if it could be some kind of compliment to dance around the room in someone's clothes, or clothes you had made out of the clothes they had discarded, crowing, Look at me! even as you're pointing at them.

Leonard had finished talking to Jaap, or Jaap to Leonard. The Dutchman put his hand on Leonard's shoulder, which Leonard seemed to take with good grace. Jaap got up and left. Leonard sat back and breathed and looked up and scanned the room. Jenny stepped backwards, almost tripping, and turned, her hand up to her hair. She put down her glass and almost ran on booted legs from the room.

10

Going to find the toilets, Jenny became lost, and found herself back near the main conference rooms. The foyer, as she slipped through it – weaved or wove through it – was quiet and empty. The toilets too were empty; the lights clicked on when she went in. She sat in a stall and peed, at length, scrolling through her phone as she did so, watching the world whisk by on her feed, setting it going again whenever it threatened to stop. She tried to gauge the volume of wine consumed from how long it took her to pee. She was, she knew, halfway to drunk, or more than halfway. Others were heading that way, but she was in the vanguard. She stayed sitting when she finished, boredly transfixed by her phone, until the lights went out, and she had to wave her arms above her head to reactivate them.

She dried herself, pulled up her knickers and then her tights, staggering somewhat in the cubicle so that she knocked into the side of it – like a caricature of a drunk woman, she thought, which only made her exaggerate further, tripping herself deliberately and swearing to herself. The stall door banged cheaply as she opened it.

She leaned over the hand basin to ogle her reflection, trying to bring it under control. She touched again at the fringe, and where her hair came down past her ears in two short, delicate, feathery blades, like birds' wings. Under the harsh light her hair felt odd to the touch, as if it were a wig. She considered her makeup, prodding nervously at her eyes, her mouth, but it was beyond recuperation, and she was beyond fixing it, and anyway everyone else was drunk, so what was the point?

'Fuck it,' she said. She pushed on the tap and washed her hands, then drank some of the featureless water and splashed some on her face, drank some more, let it drip down her chin.

Walking back past the plate-glass windows onto the courtyard, she saw there was someone out there, in the dark, two people, a pair of figures set among the shrubs and statues. It was Jaap and someone, a woman. Jenny took a step back, away from the glass and the light, and observed them. They were standing and talking; he was talking, she was listening. The woman was Lieve. She stood slyly, as if impervious to his words. Her wine glass was held up to her chin, her chin raised, her other arm crossed over her belly, holding a canvas bag to her; it must be cold out there, Jenny thought, and she wasn't wearing a coat. She was like a faun, smaller than the man she spoke to, but equipped with faculties and aspects he would have no answer to.

Jaap was smoking as he talked, but what he was saying was without meaning; Jenny knew it as surely as if she could hear it. She had heard it so many times in her life. The human chatter that was no more than birdsong: insubstantial, without issue, a statement of presence at most. What Jaap was saying had significance only insofar as it guaranteed the continued proximity of her body to his. It was the woman's listening, more than his talking, that controlled the conversation.

Jenny watched them, feeling now her knee tremble, now her eyelids thicken and sink. She was so tired, and it was not finished. And there was only so much spunk and drive she could still take from the alcohol she had drunk, and might yet drink, before fatigue and incapableness claimed her altogether. And she could not sleep until she had acted. She had to stay upright, move forward, leave her mark on the day. She needed to bring love, in some form, into her life.

There was no moon, and the man and woman were out of reach of the uplighters scattered around the courtyard. Jenny stayed there, watching, as Jaap finished his cigarette and dropped the butt to the ground. As soon as he took his eyes off her, looking down to press the butt out on the ground, she was gone, towards a door on the far side of the courtyard, leading back into the building. The professor-in-waiting let her go, only looking up when he heard the door bang to. Jenny stepped back, in case Lieve decided to come this way down the corridor, but she didn't. There was her dark form, briefly, disappearing around a different corner. Jenny waited for Jaap, slowly, to go, the same way, then she followed him, at a distance, back into the fray.

In Jenny's absence, the string quartet had disbanded and reformed itself as a band to dance to. The buffet had been cleared, apart from the coffee and desserts, and catering staff were moving the central tables to the sides of the room. The music, now amplified, had become cajoling, insistent: folk music from eastern Europe, and from a time when this music was the lifeblood of community, an essential component.

The first violin ran in loud tight reels around the few snatches of melody. The second violinist had moved to a driving semi-acoustic guitar, the cellist to an electric bass; the fourth musician had a thin wide drum that he played sideways on his knee, thrumming out a droning rhythm with his thumb and fingers. The violinist was stamping his foot as he played, giving violent jerks of his head with every bow-stroke, so his long hair bounced down over the strings.

Jenny had enjoyed the chamber music, but this offered her nothing, though she knew Frankie would enjoy it. One couple was doing a slow-mo jitterbug, another was doing the twist, with what looked like a painful irony. People clapped and cheered. Jenny watched it all in dismay, redoubled in tiredness.

She found Frankie by the profiteroles and sliced fruit.

'I was looking for you.'

'Well, good god. You've found me. Help me with this food. I can't eat it all.'

Frankie was not drunk, or barely, and Jenny knew that this put her, herself, at a disadvantage. She poured herself a coffee, and they carried their plates to a small table across the room from the music. It was loud enough that they needed to lean into each other to speak and to hear.

'You look shattered. You must be ready to collapse.'

Jenny shook her head as she lifted her cup to her mouth. She didn't know what she intended by shaking her head.

'Well, you're doing fantastically. I'd be in bed by now, no question.'

Frankie posted a morsel of tart into her mouth. Jenny couldn't find a way to say what she needed: that it was only Frankie that was keeping her awake. Once they had spoken, and whatever transpired from that had done so, she could sleep, safe in the knowledge that her life would roll on, down one side of the hill or the other.

Jenny watched her friend, how she turned and affected to watch the room as she chewed, and removed crumbs from her made-up lips with the tip of a finger. More people were dancing, in pairs, bringing themselves in close to each other, then flinging themselves apart, so their bodies jolted an arm's length from each other. It was all so exuberantly antiquated.

Frankie breathed in, pointedly. Perhaps she was thinking of the dances in her – in their – past. For they had danced, in their time. There was a love of old-fashioned dancing in the lesbian world; its tea dances, hops and late-night dives grew out of a collective nostalgia for times when these things were a vital social institution. It was a way of honouring the women of the 30s and 40s who came together in private to dance. You could be together – all of you, in a room, and the two of you, in the room you made in the room by dancing. You could drink gin and orange from china tea cups, and halves of stout, and eat olive paste on dry crackers to your heart's content. Frankie had introduced her to that world, and she had enjoyed it, for Frankie's sake, but it was not her world.

She saw Frankie's bust rise, and then settle. It was not maternal in effect, but matronly. What was hard was to marry the sense of this clothed bulwark, fixed and impregnable, with the flesh that lay beneath or behind it, fatally susceptive. Frankie's breasts, splayed as they would have been down across her body, as they lay in bed, had always been pillars of her strength. Jenny's own had only ever been boobs, tits, inconsequential puddles in comparison, barely worth mopping up.

She watched Frankie's jaw, how it slowed in the loop of chewing. She waited for what she judged to be the moment of maximum vulnerability, but without knowing to what end.

When it came, she said, 'I could kiss you.'

Frankie looked round at her. 'What did you say?' The words came through food, coarsely, just as Jenny had done, earlier. She was doing it on purpose. She was doing it all on purpose.

'I don't know. I said I could kiss you. It's true.'

'Of course it is. Of course you could.'

They sat there without speaking. Looking was like kissing, Jenny thought, when it was like this, reciprocal, and reciprocated. When you both looked, together and at once, really looked: investigating, and opening yourself up to investigation. Jenny felt her breathing climb inside her chest, felt her thoughts ride the top of it, like a boat on the swell. Her mind was churning with words. Any one of them might be the key that opened the door.

'Oh, Jenny,' Frankie said. She leaned her head back against the wall, so she was watching the room, then ran her tongue along between her teeth and her lip, as if cleaning them of food or flavour. Her hand came out and felt blindly on the table for Jenny's.

Jenny put her hand into it, and waited. She felt as if the entirety of her being was poured into that hand. It was all she was, all she had left. She let it be held, did not act with it.

When Frankie spoke again, it was to say, 'It's too late for kissing.'

Then she said, 'What's been unkissed cannot be kissed again. We're too far from the people we were.'

Finally, she looked over, and there was an access of tears behind her eyes. Jenny's own blinked in sympathy.

'And besides, you just fell into my lap.'

'Hardly.' Jenny swallowed. Her voice felt very quiet. 'You reached up and plucked me from the tree.'

'You can't fall again.'

'Are you seeing anyone?'

'Jenny Wren, am I seeing anyone? Am I seeing anyone? I'm seeing *you*. No. I have divested myself of passion. It didn't... suit the make-up of my portfolio. I took it off and left it somewhere, I can't remember where. Maybe someone else will find it. Maybe it will suit them.'

'This is hard to hear.'

'Why is it hard?'

'Because I feel it's my fault.'

The room was rank with noise. Jenny's head throbbed with it. The perky, jerky music, all hoots and elbows, was overlaid with the incoherent racket of human voices.

'You are worrying me, darling,' Frankie said. 'You don't sound like yourself. I mean, really. You can't want to start again, truly.'

'I'm not sure. Oh, I don't know.'

There were tears in her eyes, now, for real, and gravel in her throat. And, finally, Frankie did squeeze her hand. Jenny let it be squeezed. With her other hand she brushed at her idiot cheeks, this one then that one. She felt very much how the room rolled out from them. All the people, dancing and drinking and connecting. No one, it seemed, was looking at them. She was safe so long as she didn't move.

'Yes, I want to,' she said. 'I want to, desperately. I was stupid. I took myself off, like a coward, after that calamity. I thought I was being brave. I thought it would make me a better person.'

'Perhaps it has.'

'Oh, hardly. I only ever wanted to be a better person so as to be in with a chance again, with you.'

'Oh, Jenny.'

Jenny looked at her friend, but Frankie's eyes were hovering closed.

'We don't have to pretend we're teenagers any more,' Jenny said. 'We don't have to sign up for anything.'

Frankie didn't say anything in response to this. In their absence, Jenny heard the words Frankie wasn't saying, that she was reaching for and rejecting – as too close, too hard, too harsh to use. Never put yourself in the position, Jenny reflected, of having to ask for confirmation of your worst fears. She felt the room slide away from them again. She hated that she could only wait, when what she wanted was to move forward. Then Frankie opened her eyes, but instead of looking across to her, she was looking up. There was another person standing next to them, only of course it was Leonard.

'Ladies.'

'Leonard.'

'Leonard.'

He had his hand on the back of a chair, to pull out and sit with them, but Jenny realised at once that this would not do. She was beyond the point where she could bear to sit down with these two people and talk with them as if everything was fine. Instead, she stood up and took him by the hand. He looked at her, confused, and she nodded towards the music.

'You don't mind?' she said to Frankie, and her friend shook her head, her concern shading into perplexity and back again.

'It's just that Leonard might be quite tired.'

'I was coming to say goodnight, really.'

'Well, then, one last dance,' she said, jiggling his hand. 'One last dance.' And then she realised what she had said.

He showed dark amusement at her scandalised expression.

'One last dance, then,' he said to Frankie.

'And then we should go?'

'I think so.'

They began to make their way towards the music, painfully slowly. The musicians, too, had started to slow, had perhaps even done so in response to their approach. The jig they were playing eased up, took a breath, and with a deft hop and a skip it was suddenly a waltz, clement and accommodating. Leonard disengaged his hand from Jenny's, and they walked to a space on the floor that grew to welcome them, people stepping back to make room, as around the bride and groom at a wedding, though they carried on dancing, in their couples, thank god. Jenny felt herself tense at the thought that people would think this was what she had intended, to make herself the focus of attention, here at the end of the party for him.

They faced each other. He lifted one hand to shoulder level, and extended the other towards her waist, and she went forward into his loose embrace, hand in his hand, gaze looped tight round his right ear. They waited for the music to come back around, then stepped sideways into the dance.

It was acutely embarrassing. Everyone knew who he was, presumably. Plenty of people would know her. That she was quite drunk was obvious; her steps were as uncertain as his. She might turn a heel of her boot, or go at the knee altogether. She barely knew where she was putting her feet.

'Your hair,' he said, when they were settled into the rhythm. 'It wasn't like that this morning?'

'Yes, it wasn't.'

'Good. I thought I was going mad. It looks nice, though, obviously. Very smart. Very punky.'

'Thank you. And thank you for finding me.' They had accommodated themselves to the pace of the music, but still their trajectory was limited. His reserves of energy were obviously very low. It wasn't clear if they would last even the length of a waltz. They moved their feet only on every other beat, but when they did, they moved together. The most that anyone could come out of this with, she thought, was dignity. The musicians, at least, seemed to be on their side, letting the tempo slide around their movements.

'I was wondering if you'd been avoiding me.'

'I wasn't. Then I was.' She dipped her head to bring her mouth into line with his ear. The shoulder of his thin old familiar jacket was so close she could have lent her head against it. 'I didn't know,' she said. 'About you being sick. How could it be that I didn't know?'

She could see the different people and groups of people watching them, or not quite watching them, as they turned within the crowd.

'I don't know. Or I do. I chose not to tell you. You were in America. I thought I might be gone before you came back, and that seemed easier.'

'Easier?'

'For a time it was supposed to be very quick. Then it wasn't. Then this happened.' He lifted his head, a gesture that took in the whole conference. 'Frankie's idea, of course. It had been on the cards, but it was supposed to have been next year. And so it was all a bit of a rush. And I was worried what you would think.'

'What I would think?'

'That'd you be angry with me.'

'Angry?'

'For making you feel like I needed to be pitied. Or deserved it, even. I know – I mean, I remember...'

'Stop it.'

He stopped, or relented, then started to speak again.

'Shh...' She squeezed his hand that was holding hers, up there beside them in the air, as if on show.

'Jenny, please.'

'What?'

'Don't shush me. It's been a hard year. Not the illness, which you rise to. But the moral disorientation. People turn you into a bloody saint, wheel you out to your rock, your pillar in the desert. And you lap it up. There is this awful temptation to hunt down and apologise to everyone you've ever hurt, or wronged. It's monstrous. That you feel the need to make people forgive you. Can you imagine that?'

'No. Or yes. I don't know.'

'Or worse, that you feel, instinctively, not just that people will forgive you, but that they *want* to forgive you, and that you're doing them a favour by giving them the opportunity to do so. But, Jenny, I want to say it. I fucked up. With you. It's not just that it's all over the place these days, and quite right too. That makes no difference. It's more that I didn't try to make it right, when it happened. And that by doing so I sacrificed our friendship out of fear of being made to feel small. I had a million chances to apologise, and I ignored them.'

'You don't have to apologise.'

'No, but I did. I *did* have to. And, well, actually that question is not in your dispensation.'

They danced on. She felt her helplessness rise, and she realised that some of it, at least, was anger.

'It's language that betrays you, ironically enough. Cancer is the only decent word in the entire vocabulary. Everything else just makes you want to die. Bring forth trite metaphors only. Do you know what I heard myself say, only yesterday? I'm not at death's door, yet. Death's door.

'Death's door,' he said again. 'What a thing to say. Though in fact there's something heartening about it. You can't have a door with nothing on the other side, can you?' He laughed a bitter laugh. Jenny zipped her smile tight inside her mouth. What would he say next, she thought. Let it be over, soon.

He went on. 'We enter this world through the smallest door there is, but we leave it through a much larger one. Which sounds quite grand, doesn't it? Just as long as I can even get the bloody door open, when I reach it. As you can tell, I'm not good for much, these days.'

'Maybe it will be like a church door. You know. That has a smaller door inside of the larger one.'

'Maybe.'

She looked at the dancers, over his shoulder. From their playing, their unspoken conversation, she could tell that the dance was coming to an end.

'Leonard,' she said.

'Yes?'

'About tomorrow. I'd like to apologise in advance. I don't know what I'm going to say, or how I'm going to say it. It will be appalling.'

'No, I'm looking forward to it, honestly. Contingency and desire is very much what I'm all about at the moment. When every day might be your last you tend to find every gesture, every action, has the ring of contingency about it. Every bowl of cereal I eat might be the last one I eat, or might not. Every glass of beer. It's difficult to assess quite how it tastes. I've honestly never felt more subjunctive in my life.'

'No, I didn't mean that. All that stuff is fine. I mean, the stuff about you that I'm supposed to say. How to talk about you. It'll be dreadful. I mean, it'll be dreadful for you.'

'Well, it's the condemned man's privilege to forgive the executioner. He only asks that the stroke be clean and true.'

She shook her head.

'Look, Jenny. You want my advice. Or not my advice, but a request.'

The waltz came to an end. There was a smattering of applause, gentle, uncertain.

He spoke on, quietly.

'Tell them I'm dying.'

The musicians watched them, waiting to see what they would do.

'I mean, they already know. Everybody knows. But nobody will say it. Frankie wouldn't, yesterday. She said it would cast a pall over the whole thing. But tomorrow is fine. We'll be done. Just acknowledge it. Say it. As part of your speech.'

'Oh God. I don't know. I mean, I'll try.'

'Thank you. I would be most appreciative. Were you to do it, you would absolutely have my blessing.'

He took her hand in his, and made a short bow. There was some gentle laughter. She refused to look. Their dance had somehow become the culmination to the evening, a clumsy apotheosis. He lowered himself further, to bring his lips close to her hand, she felt him wobble with the strain, and she tightened the muscles of her wrist and arm, to give him something to lean on. She could see the top of his head, the mottled scalp under the thinning hair, a bald patch at its centre. The bald spot radiated immense vulnerability. And this, she thought, was the very first part of him to have seen the world. The part by which we make our entrance into the world. For an awful moment she wanted to reach out and put her hand on it, a blessing in return, like people sometimes supposedly felt the urge to reach out and touch the bellies of pregnant women.

He straightened himself, and she leaned in and pressed her lips to his cheek. As she did so she pressed down with her booted toe on the top of his shoe, pressing, pressing. She felt his hand squeeze hers, harder, harder, as if the two of them formed a circuit through which the pain could transmit itself. She pulled her lips away from his cheek, but kept herself leaning close in. He was beginning to make a noise, a low groaning. She didn't know if people could see them, could see what she was doing. She didn't care. His fingers squeezed harder and harder, until she felt she could bear it no longer, and she unpressed her boot from his toe.

She stepped back and he stepped back, and then they were just joined at the hand, where he held hers. Then Frankie was at his side, and Jenny passed him over to her. She would not look at him.

Frankie took him and moved him back through the dancers, who applauded again, all of them caught and transfixed in this moment of exquisite awkwardness. And Jenny watched them go, burning with power and shame. She felt a clench in her stomach muscles, and again, and her chest rise and the prick of water at the far reaches of her eyes. He was moving forwards, she thought. This was him, moving forwards, for what else could he do?

She stepped back, and the band leader counted in – fast again – for the next song.

11

It was only when they were gone that Jenny realised that
it wasn't just Leonard that had gone, but Frankie, too.
And how fully, and completely. She wasn't just gone with
Leonard, from out of the room. And not just for the night.
She was gone from her grasp, from her range of possibili-
ties. Irretrievably gone. Jenny stood there distraught, as the
music coiled and uncoiled around her, leaping about then
falling dead at her feet, all to no avail.

The band had picked the pace back up and were storm-
ing into the last, defiant rush of their set. The violinist
stamped his foot harder and harder. The guitarist lifted her
instrument away from her body so it stood vertical in the air
as she played it. The drummer was lurching to and fro with a
relentless, stumbling gait, bent convulsively over the sounds
he was making.

Jenny had intended to retreat quietly to the back of the
room, but was surprised to find that the other dancers
seemed ready to step in and rescue her, pulling her in to

jive and twist with them. Perhaps it showed in her face, or perhaps they thought she was bringing down the mood, but either way Jenny was happy to be co-opted. Dead on her feet one moment, the next she was being flung about like a rag doll by a series of competent young men and women. When it was announced that the next song would their last, she threw herself into the maelstrom, grabbing hands to spin and be spun, bending and thrusting out her backside and waggling it from side to side. Her dress clung to her flanks. Her arms almost jerked from their sockets.

The song ended, and everyone erupted into whooping cheers. Was this her fourth wind, or her fifth, she wondered, as she collapsed, raw-lunged and laughing, onto a chair. A beer was in her hand, there were people sat either side of her, talking across her and around her as if she was a natural part of the ongoing conversation.

They said they were going on to a bar, and she should come. She agreed, in a spirit of morbid curiosity: for who knew what state she would end up in. There is comfort, after all, in submitting to such processes, of forcing the issue, pushing through to reach one's worst fears, if only to be sure they still check out.

Then she discovered they were cycling to the bar. She didn't have a bike, she said. That wasn't a problem. Someone could give her a ride. She was too drunk, she said (and too *old*, she didn't say) but this, too, was dismissed. Everyone was fairly drunk by now. It wasn't far. It would be fine.

Then she was outside, in the cold hard Amsterdam air that, she hoped, might go some way to sobering her up. Certainly, it raked the back of her naked neck, newly exposed to the world, reminding her how she was born again. Those without bikes waited around, jiggling their arms inside their coats, while those with went to fetch them. Here they came, and here was one being reversed up to Jenny, as if she was cargo in a loading bay. She was supposed to sit on the rack at the back, something she hadn't done since she was a teenager.

Her designated driver was a tall tousle-haired postgrad student in jeans called Ingrid. They shook hands. Jenny couldn't stop her hands from shaking.

'Sorry,' she said. Now her teeth were chattering.

'Let's get you to the club,' said Ingrid. 'It will be cosy in there.'

Jenny said that was a good idea. She placed herself on the rack side-saddle, knees tucked together and feet lifted off the ground, then placed her arms cagily around Ingrid's waist.

'You good?' said Ingrid. Jenny said she was.

'Here we go,' said Ingrid, then she lifted herself up and pushed down on the uppermost pedal, setting the bike wobblingly in motion. Jenny shut her eyes and clenched her jaw, but the bike soon straightened out and began to pick up speed.

'All OK?' Ingrid called over her shoulder.

Jenny gave a yelp of uncertain meaning, and Ingrid laughed as she pedalled.

The bike hit some cobbles and Jenny heard her wailing voice bobble babyishly about, rattling her chest from the inside – a-wah-wah-waaaah – but then they turned into a bike lane and were moving smoothly and powerfully along. The bike lurched in time to Ingrid's pedalling. There was the occasional shout between cyclists, the ding of a bell. Jenny loosened her arms a little around Ingrid's waist. She was wearing a bright yellow backpack, and Jenny rested her head against it, feeling the material rub her cheek, moving up and down, up and down. She had the barest sense of the city passing them by: buildings, pedestrians, trees, dipping chain-link fences lining the canals. It was a blurred magic trick, things being whisked away before she had so much as had a chance to take them in.

When they got there, Jenny dismounted, stumbled upright and looked around herself. The journey seemed to have only taken a few minutes. In a moment of lucidity she opened her phone map and entered the name of her hotel. The red pin dropped, and there was the blue pulsing circle. They weren't far at all. They must have cycled almost right by it.

She followed the others up the stairs and inside. The bar turned out to be a club of the old-fashioned type: a social environment built around a dance floor, but not reducible to it. There were booths in red or perhaps dark brown leather, with shaded lamps fixed to the tables; the walls had framed prints, not that you could really make out what they were of, beyond vague abstraction; the lighting was low enough to console, the music not so loud that it couldn't successfully be shouted over.

Jenny bought herself a whisky and coke, then squeezed herself into a booth with Ingrid and her new friends. It seemed that most of them were Dutch postgrad students and junior lecturers, but they were happy enough to talk in English. They exchanged gossip gathered over the day. Whose presentations had been good. Who had asked dumb-ass questions. When Jaap's name cropped up Jenny nodded, but said nothing.

They asked her questions, and Jenny talked a bit about Leonard, Manchester, the past. It was easy enough. To these people, she and he were distant figures brought briefly into closer orbit by happenstance. She talked loudly and quickly, then realised she was saying more or less what she had written in the hotel, for her speech. Leonard as teacher, as someone moving obliquely through the same field of knowledge as you, clearing a path you might follow, or might simply use as a navigational aid.

They listened politely, but talking like this felt weirdly weightless, less use than riding through the city on the back of a bike. Tomorrow she would stand on the stage and say all this again, all these words or words like them, and Leonard would be there, and Frankie, too. And it was her job to tell them what they all knew but none could say: that Leonard was dying. But it was her job also to tell them what they didn't know: that she was dying, Frankie was dying, all of them were dying, dead. Dear god, she was drunk.

She finished speaking, barely knowing anymore what she'd said, except that she had drained herself of things to say, or of the power to make the things she said sound worth saying. Someone else took their turn and she cocked her head to pretend to listen. The music hammered over it. It was electronic music of a kind that she recognised: long, rather leaden constructions not really written to make people dance, and certainly not to lift their hands in the air in the joyous spirit of communal dissolution she remembered from when she used to go clubbing, in Manchester, all those years ago. It was hard dark stuff to her hearing, all bass and no drums. She did want to dance again, now, though, she thought. She wanted to wring herself ragged, after the farce of the public waltz with Leonard, shake herself clean of the muscle memory of dancing with a dead man. It was that or drop. Neither talk nor drink would do anything more for her now.

She squeezed her way out of the booth, then moved in the direction of the music, turning sideways to fit between the people standing, drinking, half-dancing. The music was squelchy underfoot, fast crisp and sticky beats, and always louder than you think. Where the dance floor began was not precisely clear, but as she neared it she began to alter the movements of her shoulders and thighs, of her trunk on her hips and her head on her neck, aligning herself to the music's directives, its burrs and slabs and blurs and stabs, so that by the time she was on the floor proper she could say with certainty that she was definitely dancing.

Plenty of other people were dancing too, but that was their business. In her heart Jenny knew that dancing was a solidly personal activity. She inserted herself into the music, letting it come at her from this side, from that side, then unpicked a thread and followed it as it unwound, letting herself move deeper into the maze, and then allowed herself to be drawn back in when it wound itself back up. She thought of the lightning zig-zags of the Bach partitas, and the jagged reel of the amplified violinist, and tried to bring them into her movement. She tried not to notice when one song ended and the next began; she yielded to the illusion that there was no music, or that the music was something to be found inside, rather than something external, to respond to. She drilled down into the dancing, struggling with it like a toddler pummelling a soft toy that won't fight back. She closed her eyes and danced, let the thud of the bass tug her about, this way and that, harum-scarum, in the dread beat room; she opened her eyes and there they were.

There they were.

It was clear that they had been there before her. For how long, she couldn't tell. She couldn't remember when she'd last seen them, back in the conference. Leonard, and the dancing, had been enough to block them out. They were at the far side of the dance floor, where it gave over again to seating and tables. She had to stand absolutely still – a challenge in itself, in this state, this dead-beat state – and squint, to be sure, but it was them. Jaap Vos and Lieve, and another girl, that she thought or guessed was the girl who'd been with her at the canal; and a boy or young man of their age or thereabouts that she didn't recognise, for why should she? He was not important.

Jenny started dancing again, but turned herself to face away from Jaap's group, so that now it looked more like she was dancing with the two people nearest her. She set up a rhythm to her movements that allowed her to send regular glances in their direction: like an automaton running through a tightly looped series of actions. First this, then that, then this, then that, and then – occasionally – this other thing, that meant she lifted an arm and turned her head, credibly, to look.

Now it was Lieve and the boy that were talking, though she seemed scarcely interested in what he had to say. It was the other girl, long-haired, Asian- or Indonesian-looking, who was dancing with Jaap – or dancing at him. She was face-on to him, moving explicitly with the music:

undulating her torso, swaying her hips from side to side and briefly locking them, this side, then that; making snakes of her arms, and raising them above her head, and moving her face from side to side, presenting her face first to this one of her two upheld arms, then to the other. The sinuous, laggy movements told Jenny that she was quite drunk.

Watching her, from this distance, and through the thick strobe of the music and the alcohol and tiredness, Jenny saw how the girl's dancing was a dumb show of sex. How it ran through an approximation of the range of movements that would occur, later, in bed. Not that anyone made these movements in bed, not really. What she was doing looked like sex, Jenny thought, still dancing, herself, in her stilted loop of moves, but sex looked nothing like that.

Jaap, dancing back at the girl, had a pitifully limited repertoire. He was, as Lieve had said, a terrible dancer. His facile jiggling seemed to want to give the impression that he was permanently on the point of beginning to dance, that at any moment he would really start. He was talking, as they danced; and he included Lieve in this, even though he had to talk over the shoulder of the sexy drunk dancing girl to do it.

Now, as Jenny watched, it appeared that something that Jaap had said, or something in his manner, had put out or annoyed the long-haired girl, woman, student. She stopped dancing and stood there, stock still, still facing him, still looking at him. The sudden change had the effect of making Jaap, still dancing, look more ridiculous. His movements, without hers to play off against, showed the full extent of their ineptitude.

Jenny looked away from them, at the man who was dancing next to her, and he smiled at her, and she smiled back and raised both her arms above her head, almost out of pity for his misguidedness, to make him feel less bad about himself. She was sweating in the dress so badly it made her laugh, and the laugh made her gulp for air. It was not a dress for dancing in. She brought her arms down and turned and looked back over – only to see the girl going, stalking off, pushing past other dancing people. Lieve looked like she was about to follow, but Jaap, through word or gesture, held her back. The girl – the long-haired girl, young woman – changed direction, so that she was coming across the dance floor, heading towards Jenny. She was coming this way.

Jenny stepped back, half-hidden at the edge of the dance floor, but the woman came past her all the same, noticing her only at the last moment, so that she half-turned as she passed her, Jenny turning too, and following her with her eyes, so as to be ready to speak or listen, to engage if it was called for, but the woman made a face, confused and dismissive all at once, and went.

Jenny returned her attention to Jaap and Lieve and the boy.

The boy, too, had gone now. It was just Jaap and Lieve, over on the far side of the dance floor. He was still dancing, his pointless, half-arsed performance, which he had to carry on with, presumably, to show he was unaffected by the girl's departure. He had a bottle of beer in one hand and he drank from that as he danced from side to side, pushing his knees forward without lifting his feet from the floor, working backwards with his elbows. He looked like someone doing competitive walking, the stupidest of all Olympic sports.

He said something to Lieve and she nodded, or shook her head. She was not really dancing, just standing, barely moving, on the spot. Jaap took a step towards her.

There were people in the way, and Jenny had to move to keep them in sight.

Now they were closer together, the two of them. They had taken up a position in relation to each other than echoed that from earlier, in the courtyard of the university building. There was no word for the stance taken up by two bodies with regards to each other in a nightclub, with the dark black set against the red. Perhaps there was a word in fencing, or ballet, but Jenny knew nothing of these things. Like the optical illusion of the vase that was also two faces facing each other, their bodies offered the viewer the choice as to which was figure and which was ground.

The shape that was the space between them was amorphous and never still, as the two of them moved, and she moved, and others moved across her line of vision, like the wax shapes in a lava lamp. The music moved through her in thudding circles, some of them short and tight, others longer. Its endless unbeginning loops led to a kind of stasis. The alcohol piled up, and the tiredness, and the dark heat of the room, and the heat under her dress. She undid the top button, and the one below that, feeling them slip like pills of bone through the wet wool. She stretched her neck and felt how sleek it was with sweat. She laid a hand against her new-cut hair, on the nape. It was wringing wet. She felt she could feel every strand of it. Everything burred and blurred around her, the music coming at her like slabs in her head, stabs in her head. She thought about Frankie, and she thought about Leonard, and she thought about how everybody in the room, every one of them there, dancing and moving, not moving forward, never moving forward, was already dying, dead, as good as dead.

bass no drums. Drum no drum no drum no drums. Hard phat bass no drum drums no beat-beat doing its thing with your drums. On the floor drums to the floor, thock to the floor, thock to the floor. Coming at you from: this from the, this from that side, inside from that side, side from that side. And louder than you think, than you think, than you can think. Louder than you think, always louder than you think. Dowder think. Dowder think beat drum think. And Everything blurs. Blurs and blurs. Everyfang burrs. Nevething urze and blurs, their furze and blurs. Fused with birds, confused with birds fused birds. And Sticky beats. Sticky beats sticky beaks sticky beats sticky bits. City child. You give me the strength. Like a toddler yelling at toy that won't flight back. A child inside a soft toy that won't fly back...

[...]

bass no drum drums. Hard phat bass no drum-beat doing its thing with your drums. On the floor drums to the floor, thock to the floor. Coming at you from: this from that side, inside from that side side from that side. And louder than you think, than you think, than you can think. Louder than you think. Dowder think. Dowder think think beat drum. Everything blurs. Blurs and blurs. Everyfang burrs. Neverthing furze and their furze and blurs, fused with birds, confused with birds they fused birds. And Sticky beats, sticky beats sticky beaks sticky beats tricky sticky bits. City child you give me the strength. Like a toddler yelling on that won't fight back. A child inside a soft toy that won't fly back still the beats, the same slabs in your ears, slabs in your ears. Those they're (what? what?) they're drilling a hole in your head. Drilling and hold in your head, in your head, drilling your head. Drilling a hole in. Drilling a hole in and hold of a hole in. Diving in. Drilling into and Diving in. Diving in your earring. Herein your hearings, here in your hearing, here in your head. Herein your head, herein your clearing, here in your head, herein your head. We're in your hearing, herein the dread. Dread beat dread beat dread beat, dread beat dread beat dread beat dread. Here in your hearing your head. Dread beat dread. Dread beat dread. Diving in your head Dread beat and dread. Diving, coming in your hearing. Squelchy underfoot, no bones no beats no bones, no drums. Squelchy underfoot. Hard dark stuff all bass, bass no drums bass no drums no bass. Drum no drums. Drum no drum no drum no drums. Hard phat stuff all bass no drums, bass no bass no drums. Drum no drum no drum no drums no drums. Hard phat bass no drum drums no beat-beat doing its thing with your drums. On the floor drums to the floor, thock to the floor. Coming at you from: this from

Then the music was stronger and the lights starker in their gaps of dark, and she felt as though she could barely see. They were speaking, Jaap and Lieve, and his movements were still the same stilted, uncertain gestures at movement, but they were made stronger, it seemed to Jenny, by the power of whatever it was he was saying. It was as if they had carved out a space within the room, a room inside the room. She, the other woman – Lieve – moved, gently, listening, but her listening was more acquiescent than before: more affirmative. Listening, she looked about herself, as if to see if her friend had indeed gone, or to check that she hadn't come back.

Jenny had a glass in her hand. Someone had bought it for her. She put it to her lips and lifted it, dancing, and the rim of it jolted her teeth, and the drink sluiced in short hard gulps down her throat.

There must be people here that knew them, she thought. This was not a darkened courtyard in the university building far from the party, with statues and hedges to hide behind. It was a time of night, and this was a place, that severely limited the available meanings, the available endings. There were fewer places left that this could go, and that seemed to Jenny a terrible thing.

Now, on a word of Jaap's, the two of them moved around the edge of the dance floor, to where it was darker still, less lighted. They were talking less; their conversation came not in words, but in looks, in curt, minimal gestures. Jaap had finished his beer. He touched her arm. Jenny watched, fixated, appalled. Lieve moved her head, raising her chin. Each looked at the other, but their eyes were not locked. They were studying each other, they were making decisions, each of them was. Two independent decisions, that might share one resolution. Going back to his house, his apartment. Or to hers. On to some other, quieter place.

Now Jaap put down his beer bottle on a table, lent in, hand on arm again; they exchanged words. Then he moved away. Lieve stayed where she was. The other girl not apparent. The boy gone. The music moved around Jenny; she was stuck in the middle of it. She watched as Jaap walked off like a drunk man, with stiff, deliberate steps, heading to the bar, or the cloakroom, or the toilet. Her heart went out to him. He knew not what he did.

Although he did, of course, he knew exactly what he was doing.

There he was. She watched him go. She had very little time. She had to bring love, somehow, back into her life.

She put down her bottle and set off across the dance floor, not dancing but walking, eyes on him as she went, then on her, waiting, then back to him. Her shoulder turned this way, then that way, cutting a path as if through the music itself, peeling it off her as she went. The people she passed were as vague as trees of kelp reaching up from the dim silted sea floor.

Do you know what you're doing? It was Frankie's voice, but not just Frankie's. Her husband's too. Her mother, and her sister, she felt their hands on her as she went, felt them on either side of as she made her way through them, everyone from whose grip she had wriggled, escaped. You can only move forward. Sometimes you can only pitch yourself forward, reach out and grab at something, if only to steady yourself, or if not to steady yourself then to take out and obliterate the very thing you hoped would hold you.

She quickened her steps, like someone moving towards a precipice, towards the one decision that would realign her life, set it more securely in motion. She knew what she had to do.

12

Jenny slept. As she slept she dreamed she was asleep at the bottom of the ocean, and that she knew nothing but the fact she was sleeping and could do nothing about it. She felt the swells and currents of furious pain move, slowly and severely, far above her. Down here the water was cold and dark, and the creatures that traversed it were at once monstrous and indistinct. The weight of the water piled on top of her was the weight of the previous night, in all its confusion and sure damnation. There was land nearby, she sensed, but to reach it she would have to drag herself out of her watery grave, and she would have to grow limbs and lungs and strong bones to do so. It would hurt, like it hurt the mermaid in the fairy tale – an allegory of alcohol abuse and hangover if ever there was one.

Then she was no longer at the bottom of the sea. And no longer asleep. The first thing she saw, when she saw any-thing at all, was a band of grey laid flat across the air some uncertain distance away. She stared at that for a while, or let it be stared at, until it revealed itself as a patch of ceiling by the windows where the light came in over the top of the curtains. It was a messenger from the day to come, a day with its own, different set of confusions and damnations. The tide of the day was still far out, it said, but it would come in. That's the problem with apocalypse, thought Jenny, running a tongue round the walls of her mouth, beer- and wine-lacquered. It's rarely actually the end of anything.

I was angry, she thought. She allowed the idea to bubble up, as from a vent in the ocean floor, and the pain of the thought matched its purity. I was angry at this woman, Lieve, for falling for his spiel – for he had a spiel for her, she was sure, as he had had a spiel for Jenny. She was angry at her for being naive, for walking clear-eyed straight into it.

And yet one day he, Jaap Vos, would be dying of something. This much was certain.

No less than Leonard Peters.

And this – the two of them, the two twos of them, Jaap and Lieve, Jenny and Leonard, teacher and doctoral student, teacher and junior colleague, a shag at a conference, a quick fuck at the first post-divorce Christmas party – was something that, if it didn't happen, would one day be regretted, another notch for the great uncountable lifelong tally of regrets. And so she was angry at her, at the student, for as good as walking into the same mistake she now thought perhaps she wished she'd made, twenty years ago. For Leonard was dying, and it was a comfort, to herself, to goad herself with the thought that if she had slept with him, that one time, his death might be in some small way diminished.

Have I got that right? she wondered.

Or, she had been angry at Leonard, for making her think

about all of this, about how every word and gesture offered towards another person is a gesture that only beckons death, that catches its attention and brings it closer, like a predator that senses movement, that you can only avoid by keeping absolutely still, doing nothing, staying at home in bed, the covers over your head, not so much as breathing.

The only pain of death, she thought, the only thing that you do take with you through the door that is death, the only thing you can't leave behind on the threshold, on the mat where you take off your shoes, is regret.

Or she was angry at Jaap, for forcing her to offer herself up as sacrificial victim or martyr, to insert herself as the clarifying element into a volatile situation. Why did *she* have to act, to head off an act of his? Why was it her responsibility to save him from himself, to stop him as she had stopped Leonard?

She emitted a groan, that began in her chest and didn't really rise from there, never reached her mouth. Just sat there in her rib cage, sounding out her internal cavities.

It was met by another groan.

They harmonised briefly, two low drones, before Jenny cut hers off.

The other groan ended in a short deep briefly painful laugh.

Jenny laboriously turned her body over to face what she knew was there: the body in the bed, wrapped in the rucked and fucked-in bedclothes. This other body turned too and resolved itself to a face, with hair and a nose and mouth, and a pair of eyes.

They looked at each other.

The grey on the ceiling had begun to dissolve; it shed its grains of pale light across the bed, across its sheets mapped with valleys and ruts and folds. And across the people in it, across them, too.

'Good morning,' she said.

The voice wore its foreignness like a mist that hung over canals and low-lying fields, canals and fields that were, after all, quite close at hand. That weren't scary or empty, but full of meaning, as yet unrevealed.

'Good morning,' Jenny replied.

'Well, this is a surprise.'

'Is it?'

'I don't know. Maybe not.'

'Maybe. Maybe not.'

The words, being useless, crumbled into dust and silent mirth.

They held each other's gaze. The two gazes became a shared thing, held in common, held taut between them. Their eyes lunging and flickering, searching and sending and receiving, a thousand times a second, and who knew what information they found.

'I feel I should introduce myself,' Jenny said. 'Introduce myself properly, I mean. I'm Jenny.'

'How do you do, Jenny. It's very nice to meet you.'

'Likewise.'

Jenny untangled a hand from the bedclothes and reached it out, and the hand was met with another hand, that slowly pushed its fingers into hers until it was hard to tell whose hand was whose. The fingers interlocked and entwined, and then they extricated themselves, and placed themselves against each other, palms flat and pressing, while the two other hands began movements of their own, explorations of their own, all absolutely in the manner of these things.

ACKNOWLEDGEMENTS

Thanks to Hannah Marije Altorf and Jennifer Harvey for their comments on the manuscript. Thanks to Victor Schiferli and Nederlands Letterenfonds for the chance to stay at the Vertalershuis in Amsterdam during the writing of the book. At Boiler House Press, thanks to Philip Langeskov, Nathan Hamilton, Jasmin Kirkbride, Emily Benton, and Kristy Campbell for the typographic pages. And thanks to Susan Tomaselli, who published my short story 'Festschrift' in Gorse magazine, out of which this larger work unexpectedly grew.